"Well, that didn't seem **Dr. Seymour. I wonder** whether your problem down to a lack of assertiveness. Or perhaps you weren't in a hurry."

Beth found his unremitting and unjust criticism more than she could handle. She paused for a moment before replying. She wanted to gather the last shreds of composure she possessed. Australia was supposed to be different. A new start, where she would be valued as a doctor, and also as a person. She had to make that clear now.

Finally, with a calm that belied her still shaky confidence, she challenged her aggressor. "You're wrong with both suggestions, Dr. Harrison. It appears that Australian men are not astute enough to get the message when it's delivered politely. But don't worry. I'm sure I can alter my delivery to suit the occasion. I learn quickly."

She watched as the corners of his mouth curved slightly. Not a full smile, but Beth was relieved to see that at least wasn't the face of a man about to end her medical career. In fact, to her surprise, she found herself thinking it was a very handsome, almost roguish face. The blue eyes that had threatened her only minutes before now seemed to sparkle as they lingered on hers. She felt her pulse quicken and blood flow into her cheeks.

Conscious of her blushing, she abruptly turned her gaze from him, trying to concentrate on her case notes, but still she felt strangely distracted by his presence so close to her.

Matthew liked her spirit. She had just stood up to him, and not many people could do that. They cowered to his seniority and his reputation. But Beth didn't flinch when she gave back as good as she got.

"OD in Priority One," called a nurse as she raced past them.

Beth felt a firm hand on her arm.

"Well, Dr. Seymour, let's see just how fast you learn!"

Dear Reader,

I am so excited to introduce Beth and Matthew in my very first book, *Unlocking the Doctor's Heart*. I feel so privileged to be able to bring these characters to you and tell their very special love story.

The fact that I am able to do this as a Harlequin® Medical Romance™ author is a very special story, too. An incurable romantic, and an avid reader of Harlequin books, I have wanted to write for this publisher for the longest time. I started writing romance a few years ago and, although I did occasionally dare to dream of one day using the title of Harlequin author, I wasn't totally convinced that it would actually happen. But, just like falling in love, it happens when you least expect it.

I continued writing because I can't imagine not doing it. And, having a medical background, I wanted to write a romance set in a busy hospital. So that is just what I did—and I added the element of traveling around the world to find love. Beth is a young Englishwoman with a feisty spirit and a desire to find her own identity and fall in love, and she travels to Australia in search of both. Matthew is a man who needs love but has locked away his heart after being badly hurt. They are two wonderful people who have never found "the one." When I felt sure that this story was finally "the one" I sent it off. And then it happened. I received the call from Harlequin with the exciting offer of a book contract.

I am thrilled that my first book is set in my hometown of Adelaide, in a fictitious hospital, the Eastern Memorial. It is loosely based on a large city teaching hospital, and the story includes local landmarks, including my favorite shopping destination of Rundle Street. I hope you enjoy the roller-coaster ride that takes these two wonderful, dedicated doctors from colleagues to lovers and manages to mend a broken heart along the way.

Warmest wishes,

Susanne

UNLOCKING THE DOCTOR'S HEART

Susanne Hampton

HARLEQUIN® MEDICAL ROMANCE™

Recycling programs
for this product may
not exist in your area.

ISBN-13: 978-0-373-06954-5

UNLOCKING THE DOCTOR'S HEART

First North American Publication 2014

Copyright © 2014 by Susanne Panagaris

Printed in U.S.A.

HARLEQUIN®
www.Harlequin.com

UNLOCKING THE DOCTOR'S HEART
is Susanne Hampton's debut title for
Harlequin® Medical Romance™!

This book is dedicated to Peter, Ori, Tina and all of my wonderful family and friends who have supported this dream of mine for so long: Sylva, Yvette and Sandra, my very first homegrown editors; The South Australian Romance Authors and Romance Writers of Australia for all of their encouragement; Flo Nicoll for her amazing patience, guidance and advice.

And finally to my brother Rod—always a hero in my eyes

CHAPTER ONE

'Do I LOOK like a mop?'

Beth wondered if this was a trick question, considering the young man asking was quite tall and wiry, not unlike a stick in stature, with a head of loose brown curls. She resisted the temptation to acknowledge an odd similarity.

'Pardon me?' she asked.

'I'm sick and tired of Harrison cleaning the damned floor with me. I tell you, he treats residents like they're not fit to be in his godlike presence.'

Beth watched from the corner of her eye as the stranger paced the lift. Adding an exaggerated depth and hint of sarcasm to his voice, he continued, 'And short of lying comatose in ICU, there's no excuse for arriving late at work while I'm in charge!'

Beth turned around to fully face the figure sharing her lift. 'Please tell me you're

not talking about Dr Harrison, the senior
A and E consultant?'

'Afraid I am.'

'I was hoping—'

'Well, you're out of luck,' he cut in. 'The
other consultants are saints compared to our
Hannibal Harrison.'

The lift stopped on the third floor, the
doors opened to an empty lobby and after a
prolonged wait slowly closed again.

'Why do people push the button for every
lift on the floor?' the lanky man growled,
before giving in to a lopsided smile. 'Better
watch my temper, I'm starting to sound like
Harrison!'

Beth breathed a heavy sigh. This man had
just confirmed the rumours she had overheard when she'd visited the human resource
department only minutes before. She had
tried to dismiss it as idle gossip.

'That's just wonderful,' she said. 'I start
work with him this morning.'

'So you're the newest victim.' He smiled
sardonically, rubbing his hands, then offered
one in friendship. 'Just joking, it's a bad habit
of mine that you'll have to get used to. I'm
Dan Berketta, and you must be our RMO
exchange from London. Let me be the first

from Cas to welcome you to the Eastern Memorial.'

Beth met his handshake. 'Beth Seymour.'

The lift stopped again, this time on the first floor.

'This is where I get off,' Dan explained. 'I've been sent on an errand by the man himself. I'll catch up with you later.'

The doors closed, leaving Beth and her thoughts alone as she travelled down to the ground floor. Somehow she had to make the best of it, despite Dan's bleak report and terrible impersonation. She had no choice, she mused as the lift came to a stop. In vain she tried to tuck back a wisp of hair that escaped from her chestnut plait. She sighed when another frizzy strand fell across her eye. The humid Australian summer weather was playing havoc with her curls and that was just what she didn't need. She feared frizzy curls around her face made her look even younger and she wanted desperately to appear every bit of her twenty-eight years today.

After a few moments struggling with the rebellious wisp, she conceded defeat and stepped from the elevator into the commotion of the A and E department. It was only eight o'clock on a Monday morning, but the tone of the day ahead was evident.

The hallway was lined with chairs and each one was taken. The cries of a colicky baby were almost drowned by the abusive yelling of an elderly drunk, who was being escorted to the exit door by two well-built orderlies. A barouche, attended by three hospital staff and clearly heading for Emergency Theatre, rushed past, forcing Beth to take two steps back.

'Chin up, Beth Seymour,' she muttered to herself. 'No matter what, this is definitely where you want to be.'

Beth had worked too hard and waited too long for this day—travelling halfway around the world in the process—to let anything dampen her enthusiasm. Not even an A and E consultant with a supposed foul temper.

No one could be that bad, she decided. Or could they, she wondered, as she spied a man drumming his fingers impatiently on the reception desk. She checked her watch, even though she knew she wasn't late, then berated herself silently for letting him intimidate her before they had even met. She had made a pledge to herself to appear the consummate second-year resident, confident and totally professional.

She had recognised Dr Harrison from the description given by the girl in Personnel.

Tall, late thirties, wavy dark hair and deep blue eyes. He fitted the description, although she wouldn't have called him exceptionally tall. Height was such a personal thing, she decided as she drew closer. She couldn't help but notice his white coat was a little worse for wear as she breathed a sigh and stretched out her hand.

'You must be Dr Harrison. They told me I'd find you here. I'm Elizabeth Seymour, the new exchange resident. Everyone calls me Beth. I've been assigned to A and E.'

The man didn't meet her handshake. He stared blankly as he rubbed his chin. 'Listen, lady, I'm no doctor, I'm a dental technician. I work down the road at the dental hospital and I've been waiting for an hour for someone to take a look at my rash. I have a truckload of dentures and crowns I gotta get back to, so can you cop a squiz and give me somethin' for the itch?'

Beth dropped her hand. She was stunned into an embarrassed silence.

'Well, you heard the man,' came a voice from behind her. 'Bay four is empty, so show the gentleman in there and check out his rash, Dr Seymour.'

Beth spun around, and was forced to raise not only her eyes but her face, in order to meet the deep blue pools belonging to the voice.

It was painfully clear—in fact, Beth thought she could almost bet her future medical career on it—that this voice and these very deep blue eyes belonged to the real A and E consultant. A quick glance down at his ID tag confirmed her nightmare. The name Matthew Harrison was glaring back at her in bold print from beneath his photograph.

'Is this a hearing problem or an attitude problem, Dr Scymour?' he asked dismissively, as he sifted through some case notes on the desk. 'I said you can take this patient into bay four and begin the examination, unless of course there's some quaint English tradition that prevents you working before ten in the morning.' His eyes lifted from the case notes before him and he met Beth's stunned gaze.

'And if that's the case, Dr Seymour, you'd better see me in my office, because I don't need a second-year resident working for me but abiding by her own set of rules.'

With that he turned away, gathered an armful of files and proceeded down the hall and out of sight.

Beth bit the inside of her cheek as she looked around. The waiting room was full.

People without seats were leaning against the walls. Then there was the queue she had passed moments before in the corridor. And all of them, she felt certain, had heard the dressing down she had just received.

'Here are his notes, Dr Seymour. I've just completed them now,' said a nurse, who Beth couldn't have recognised five minutes later in a line-up if her life had depended on it. Her normally clear reasoning had deserted her the moment Matthew Harrison had attacked.

Somehow she managed to hear the end of the instructions '…and the bay Dr Harrison suggested is second on the left.'

'Fine,' Beth replied, as she took the file and tried to focus on the name. 'Well, then, Mr Somers, if you'll follow me, I'll see what I can do.'

With a bowlegged gait, he followed her. 'I sure hope you can give me something to stop the itching. It's been driving me mad for near on four days.'

With her back to the patient as she led him into the bay, Beth rolled her eyes and gave a little sigh. This was not how it was supposed to happen. The fantasies of her first day on the job in Adelaide had been very different.

She put down the notes, closed the curtains and crossed to the washbasin. Quickly but thoroughly she washed her hands and slipped on some latex gloves. Then she turned back to catch her patient drop his pants to the floor and bend over the examination table. She swallowed hard as she approached the splayed figure.

'Where exactly is the problem, Mr...? Mr...?' Oh, God, she couldn't believe she'd forgotten his name. Her eyes were levelled at a man's naked backside and she had no recollection of his name. Whether it was the sight before her or the run-in with Dr Harrison that had blanked her mind, she wasn't sure.

'Somers,' he called over his shoulder, 'Barry Somers. But my friends call me Bazza.'

'Yes, of course. Mr Somers,' she repeated, but had no need to ask where the problem was, as she watched him raise his hand to the afflicted area.

'It's just here. I was out shooting with me mates when I got nature's call and ducked behind some bushes. Well, seems like I backed into some prickly pear. I was a bit embarrassed to come in, I thought maybe it'd go away but it hasn't.'

Beth proceeded with the delicate examination. Upon completion she removed her gloves and wrote out a script.

'You can have this filled down the corridor at Pharmacy,' she explained. 'Apply the cream to the irritated area three times a day and you should be fine in a few days.'

He stared at her without answering.

'Mr Somers, did you understand me?'

'Yep,' he said. Dismissing everything else she had previously told him, he continued, 'You know, Doc, you sure are pretty. Has anyone told you that you have beautiful brown eyes?'

'Mr Somers, please get dressed.'

'Are you single?'

Beth chose to ignore the question. 'I don't mean to hurry you up but we're very busy so if you could please put on your trousers and make your way to Pharmacy.'

'Can't blame a man for asking,' he said, as he tucked in his shirt and finished dressing. 'You're from the UK, right? Been out here long?'

'Yes, I'm English and, no, I've only just arrived.' Beth answered the less personal questions. 'Now, unless there's anything related to your treatment, I think you can go.'

'Me and me mates, we've got a shack on the Murray River... Have you ever been water-skiing?'

'I'm not a watersports kind of person,' Beth replied, as she filled in the last of the case notes and closed the file. She moved to the curtain, pulling it open. 'Now, I really do have a lot of patients to see.'

'What about coffee in town one night, maybe a movie?'

As she opened her mouth to refuse his offer and to call for an orderly, a deep voice echoed behind her.

'Dr Seymour, I think I can safely speak on behalf of the rest of the hospital staff, including management and the board, in telling you that we would be eternally grateful if you would arrange your private life in your own time. There's a roomful of people waiting for treatment, if you haven't noticed, and if you stop to chat with all the male patients who flatter your ego, I'm afraid we could risk some of the others up and dying on us!'

He turned to walk away, then paused in mid-step. 'Quite frankly, Dr Seymour, I wasn't keen about this RMO exchange. It's an irritating disruption to a busy department and from what I've seen this morning, I doubt I'll be convinced otherwise.'

'I... I...' Beth fell over her own words with nerves. 'I was just trying to explain to Mr...' It had happened again. Her mind went inexplicably blank. It never happened to her. She was always in control, remembering names had never been an issue. *What was happening?* Her composure had suddenly taken a leave of absence.

'Mr Somers,' the A and E consultant added snidely, looking at the case notes under Beth's arm. 'And, Dr Seymour, try to remember names. It's a professional touch we encourage Down Under.'

'As I was saying,' she returned quickly, 'I was just explaining to Mr Somers that he needed to go to Pharmacy.'

'Well, the message wasn't getting through, was it?' he replied curtly. Then with his dark brows knitted and his arms folded across his ample chest, he stared in silence at the patient. Beth wasn't sure whether it was his towering stature or threatening demeanour, but something made Mr Somers move quickly through the gap in the curtains and out of sight.

'Well, that didn't seem so difficult, Dr Seymour. I wonder whether we should put your problem down to a lack of assertiveness. Or perhaps you weren't in a hurry.'

Beth found his unremitting and unjust criticism more than she could handle. She paused for a moment before replying. She wanted to gather the last shreds of composure she possessed. Australia was supposed to be different. A new start where she would be valued as a doctor and also as a person. She had to make that clear now.

Finally, with a calm that belied her still shaky confidence, she challenged her aggressor. 'You're wrong with both suggestions, Dr Harrison. It appears that Australian men are not astute enough to get the message when it's delivered politely. But don't worry, I'm sure I can alter my delivery to suit the occasion. I learn quickly.'

She watched as the corners of his mouth curved slightly. Not a full smile, but Beth was relieved to see it at least wasn't the face of a man about to end her medical career. In fact, to her surprise, she found herself thinking it was a very handsome, almost roguish face. The blue eyes that had threatened her only minutes before now seemed to sparkle as they lingered on hers. She felt her pulse quicken and blood flow into her cheeks. Conscious of her blushing, she abruptly turned her gaze from him, trying to concentrate on her case notes, but still she felt strangely distracted by his presence so close to her.

Matthew liked her spirit. She had just stood up to him, and not many people could do that. They cowered to his seniority and his reputation, but Beth hadn't flinched when she'd given back as good as she'd got.

'OD in Priority One,' called a nurse as she raced past them.

Beth felt a firm hand on her arm. 'Well, Dr Seymour, let's see just how fast you learn!' He directed her into the corridor and with hasty steps they followed the nurse.

'I can learn while running. I hope that's fast enough.'

Matthew gave a wry smile, which she took as affirmation. Without further debate she followed him into a room filled with nursing staff and an attending doctor already working on stabilising the patient. Beth recognised the young doctor from the lift. It was Dan Berketta.

The young male patient he was attending lay on the barouche looking deathly pale. An intravenous line had already been inserted into his forearm and as the patient was unconscious Dan inserted a Guedal airway to prevent the patient's tongue from obstructing his airway. One nurse took over the bag resuscitation while another cut down the length of his shirt. With the patient's bare torso exposed, Dan immediately began cardiac compression.

'Suspected scenario, Dr Berketta?' asked

Matthew Harrison as he put on latex gloves and threw a pair across to Beth.

'Heroin overdose, the girlfriend told us,' Dan replied, his voice gritting with the force he exerted on the patient's chest. 'The paramedics administered oxygen and Narcan en route. He was here five minutes when he ripped the IV out and attempted to leave. He made it about three feet before he arrested on the floor.'

'Still no pulse,' said a nurse.

Beth moved closer to offer assistance as Dan continued with the compressions.

'No improvement,' came the nurse's update.

Immediately Dan reached for the defibrillator paddles, his eyes constantly returning to the heart monitor.

'Everyone stand back,' instructed Dr Harrison.

The nurse already had the paddles smeared with conducting paste.

'Now!' Dan held the paddles to the man's chest. The young man's back arched with the surge they generated.

Eyes turned to the heart monitor. Still no beat registered. 'Increase to three hundred.'

'Three hundred,' the nurse confirmed.

'Clear again,' Dan called as he threw his

weight behind the pads once more. The man's body convulsed with the force.

'We have a trace,' the nurse called.

'Competent work, Dr Berketta,' Beth heard Dr Harrison say, as he reached for the patient's chart. 'But let's not be overly confident yet. Get someone from Cardiology down here to see him. I want five-minute obs, full biochem and haematology work-up and a drug screen, and one of the nurses should let the girlfriend know we'll be holding onto lover boy for at least twenty-four hours. Let's just hope he used a clean needle.'

'Bit late for that,' said Dan, slipping off his disposable gloves and untying his surgical gown. 'The blood results from his last OD are in his file. He's hep C positive. Not that he knows yet. According to his notes, he's been out of the country and they haven't been able to make contact.'

'I'll leave it in your hands, Dr Berketta, but arrange for a counsellor to be present when you inform the patient of his condition,' the consultant cautioned.

Beth closed her eyes for a moment and clenched her trembling hands. She didn't even know the man on the barouche but an incredible anger swept over her. She couldn't help but notice his expensive clothing and conservative haircut. He wasn't a street junkie. Everything about him was in conflict with the popular image she'd once had of a heroin addict.

As she watched him lying there with an oxygen mask covering his pallid face, Beth controlled her impetus to shake him to his senses. To ask him why he was throwing away his life. To find out what drove him to do it. What void was he filling with drugs? Beth found it so sad and so frustrating.

She felt a firm hand on her shoulder and turned her eyes to see Dr Harrison's face lowered to her level as he spoke. 'Had any contact with ODs during your training, Dr Seymour?'

'Too much, I'd say.' She had seen so many young lives destroyed by drugs. It seemed to be almost an epidemic during her training in London—including one of her fellow medical students, who had been a close friend all through school.

'It's a sad fact of life in the city.'

'And that means it's acceptable?' she retorted loudly, a little too loudly, she quickly realised.

'No, but it means there's nothing you or I can do except patch them up and let them get back on the street to score their next hit.

Although,' he paused '…by the look of the manicure and haircut on this one, he's a corporate user. A yuppie with a habit.'

Beth felt her body stiffen. His words cut deeply as she thought back to her friend who'd been three weeks away from graduating when he'd overdosed. 'It's a stupid waste of a life and we get to clean up the mess they leave behind.'

Matthew observed his new medical colleague as she stood deep in thought. She obviously had strong views about what she had witnessed and she wasn't afraid to come out with what she thought. Despite her small stature, she was neither a walkover nor a wallflower. She was forthright and almost commanding. It was a refreshing change.

He also noticed she was pretty, a fresh, natural beauty. He hoped despite her somewhat innocent looks she would be equipped to handle the rigours of A and E. First appearances would lead him to believe she would do just fine but perhaps treating her harshly while she might be suffering from jet lag had not been entirely fair. Despite her almost palpable anger at the situation, she looked truly shaken.

Her thoughts were interrupted by a gentle tap on her shoulder and words she hadn't expected. 'Dr Seymour, maybe I was a bit hard on you earlier.'

Beth stared in silence.

'I'm offering an apology for my previous behaviour. Make the most of it because, believe me, it's not something I do very often.'

She couldn't believe her ears—this seemed totally out of character, given everything she had heard about the man and the callous way he had treated her earlier.

'Look, the truth of the matter is I've had a lousy morning. What with one resident off sick and a fourth-year medical student tagging behind me like Casper, I guess I took it out on you.'

'There's no need—' Beth began.

'No, it's your first day here, I could have shown some empathy. Let's face it, you shouldn't think of me as an absolute son of a—' He stopped in mid-sentence. For some strange reason, and against his better judgement, he actually cared what Beth thought of him. 'Well, let's say you shouldn't completely despise me, like the rest of them do, until at least your second week here.'

CHAPTER TWO

IT WAS ABOUT seven o'clock in the evening when Beth headed for the doctors' lounge. Vivian, an attractive ashen-haired nurse who had arrived for the afternoon shift, convinced her of the need to take a tea break.

Beth had managed to slip away in the afternoon for half an hour for lunch and that had doubled as time to put her feet up. But that had been almost six hours ago and she could feel the hunger in her stomach starting to stir. The thought of waiting for the lift or walking up three flights of stairs to the staff cafeteria after ten hours on her legs had her slip some coins into the slot of a vending machine and retrieve two chocolate bars for her late supper.

'You're not setting a good example to the patients. What happened to the three well-balanced meals a day?'

Beth was stopped in her tracks by the same dogmatic voice that had started her day.

'You'd be better off with some fruit or at least a protein bar,' Dr Harrison continued before she had the chance to reply.

Trying hard to keep her heavy legs from collapsing, she turned to him. Then she wished she hadn't. He stood before her in a dark grey suit and crisp white cotton shirt, which contrasted starkly against his tanned skin and black wavy hair, which he wore slicked back. This further emphasised his softly chiselled features. A red silk tie and highly polished leather shoes completed his outfit.

Beth drew a steadying breath. He looked gorgeous and she felt like nothing on earth. She glanced down at her creased slacks and shapeless consulting coat with iodine splatters and wanted to disappear into an invisible black hole in the tiled floor. She had long since given up on her hair and had just let the curly wisps take on a direction of their own. How unfair was nature to let him bounce back and look so good after a full day's work? The musky scent of his cologne stirred senses she had thought were asleep.

'A night on the town?' she enquired as she tried to stifle a yawn.

'A celebration of sorts, actually.'

'Well, I hope you have a nice time,' she answered softly.

'I will if my date turns up on time.'

Beth thought better of staying around chatting to the handsome consultant. If he was anything to set standards by, his date would be ravishing, and after the long day she had put in she'd rather not be introduced. She would only feel like the third, and definitely shabby, wheel.

'Well, if you'll excuse me,' she began, 'I'll be going. I've only got a few minutes' break and I really need to sit down.'

'Certainly,' he said, giving her a sideways glance. 'You look like you could do with the rest.'

Beth just smiled and headed for the doctors' lounge. *You look like you could do with the rest*, she repeated in her mind. Why hadn't he just said, 'God, you look awful' and be done with it?

As she made her way down the corridor, she heard the seductive tone of his voice, then a soft female laugh. Unable to hide her curiosity, Beth turned her head and watched as a tall blonde, wrapped in a strapless red evening gown, slipped her arm through Dr Harrison's. Beth felt a stab of envy. She wasn't sure whether it was the woman's disgustingly expensive designer dress and jewelled shoes or the man with her that really appealed. Then she laughed to herself at how terrible she would look with either after such a long day, and she headed into the lounge for a much-needed half-hour rest.

To her dismay, the vision in the dinner suit filled her mind. Looking that good, she decided, should be a crime. Then she thought back to their meeting that morning, and despite his arrogant attitude Beth couldn't deny her unexpected and unwanted attraction to her boss. He was handsome and inherently sexy, that was undeniable... But there was something else. She wasn't sure what intrigued her about the man but as she felt her eyes slowly closing, she shook her weary head and climbed to her feet. Now was not the time to drift off to some pleasant reverie about her picture-perfect boss. The last thing she needed was to be found sleeping on the job.

Beth stretched her aching muscles and made her way back to A and E. She had not quite reached the swing doors when her beeper went off. The sound of hurrying footsteps in the opposite direction signalled an emergency arrival. Beth rushed through the doors and fell in step with the paramedics and the barouche. A nurse hurriedly attached a stand to the drip that one paramedic held.

'What do we have?'

'Female, hit and run, ten years of age. Vital signs okay, BP ninety over fifty, suspected fractures both legs. No other signs of injury. We've administered pethidine, IV, for pain relief.'

'Bay five,' Vivian called.

Beth nodded, then turned her attention back to the paramedic. 'Parents?'

'No, she was alone at home. A neighbour saw the accident and called us. Apparently she was looking for her cat and ran onto the road. Her name is Tania Grant.'

Beth smiled down at the young girl. 'Well, then, Tania, apart from your legs, does it hurt anywhere?'

The child's eyes glistened with tears as she shook her head.

'Okay, I don't want you to worry about anything. I'm going to have a look and make sure there's nothing else wrong while nurse Vivian tries to contact your parents.' Beth gloved up while the paramedics parked the barouche in the bay.

'Now, Tania,' she began softly, 'do you know where your parents are tonight?'

'Yes, they always go to the same place to eat on special occasions.'

'Do they often leave you alone when they go out at night?' Beth asked as she reached for her stethoscope.

'No, never… That's cold!' she protested when the metal touched her chest.

'Sorry, sweetie, but I need to listen to your heart for a minute. While I do, could you tell the nurse where she can contact your parents?'

The tall, ashen-haired nurse reached into her pocket for a notebook and pencil and jotted down the name of the restaurant. 'I'll go and call them.'

Satisfied with the child's vital signs, Beth turned her attention back to the injured legs. 'Now, Tania, I'm going to need an X-ray of both of your legs to see what damage you have and a couple of other pictures while we're there. I'd like to wait for Mummy's and Daddy's—'

'He's my stepdad,' the girl cut in.

'Fine, your mummy's and your stepdad's permission, but I don't think they'd mind under the circumstances, so as soon as nurse Vivian gets back, she'll take you around to the X-ray department and I'll see you back here in just a little while.'

Tania nodded. Beth smiled as she brushed a stray wisp of blonde fringe from the little girl's forehead. 'So you're not left alone often?'

'No, this is the first time. My stepbrother, Tom, was supposed to be home with me, but his friend who lives next door called and asked him over to watch videos. I didn't want to act like a baby and make him stay with me. If Mittens hadn't sneaked out when Tom left, I wouldn't be in this trouble.' She started to cry.

'Shh,' Beth said gently. 'You're not in trouble, but I suspect Tom might be.' She reached for Tania's file, noted her vital signs and wrote a request for X-rays. 'Vivian shouldn't be much longer, I'm sure, then you'll go straight around to Radiology.'

'But I want my mummy with me.'

'Well, let's hope she can make it here in time.'

No sooner had she finished than Vivian walked into the room and over to Tania. She patted the little girl's hand. 'Your parents are on their way. They said they'd be here as fast as they could, but the restaurant is in the foothills so it could take twenty minutes.' Then she turned her attention to Beth. 'Dr Seymour, her parents gave consent for any diagnostic tests and treatment that you feel are necessary, so I called Radiology and they're waiting for Tania. Oh, and Dr Huddy told me to let you know your shift is finished. He'll take over in here.'

'I'm sorry, Tania, we can't really wait for Mummy,' Beth replied as she gently put another pillow under the child's arm to support the IV. 'But Vivian will take really good care of you and a lovely doctor called Simon will be treating you when you get back.'

The girl burst into tears. 'I don't want to see someone else,' she sobbed, and tried to tug at her wrist where the intravenous line had been inserted and taped. 'I want you to take this thing out of my hand. It's hurting me and I want my mummy.'

Beth encircled the little girl's hands in her own. 'I know it's uncomfortable, sweetie, but the medicine in the bag up there is helping to stop the pain in your legs.' She wiped the tears from Tania's cheeks with a tissue. 'Mummy will be here very soon, and then you'll feel much better.'

Beth glanced down at her watch. She was almost past exhaustion but she was loath to leave the girl so distraught.

'How about I take you around for that X-ray, then we can wait together for your parents and you can tell me about Mittens. You know, I had a cat when I was your age but about the worst she did to me was give me a bad scratch. She certainly never put me into hospital!'

Tania gave a little smile and agreed to go with Beth for the X-ray.

It was almost two hours before Beth was able to finally leave the hospital. Tania's parents had arrived while she'd been in Radiology and Beth thought she had been so long with the little girl, she may as well stay a little longer while the orthopaedic registrar viewed the X-rays and made his decision. Beth admitted to herself that on a level somewhere between incredibly tired and flat-out exhaustion it felt good to be needed. She was making a difference just by being there, and that was a wonderful feeling. It had been such a long time since she had felt that she was important or needed by anyone.

She explained the situation to Mr and Mrs Grant and thought she would leave quietly, until she noticed how worried Tania was about the casts.

Beth remained with the family for the procedure, then accompanied them to the paediatric ward. Finally it was time to go home. Intending to catch a cab in front of the hospital, she grabbed her things and rushed through the front door of A and E—straight into Dr Harrison.

'Don't you think you're carrying dedication to the extreme?'

'It was a special case,' Beth answered, 'but I must go, I'm really past being tired. Damn!' she moaned as she saw the last cab on the rank pull away. Now she had to call another one and hope there wasn't a long wait. She opened her purse, searching for her phone. The air was still warm and although Beth hadn't been outside all day she knew it must have been a hot day to still be this warm so late in the evening.

'Did I miss something here?'

'No, but I did. The last cab,' she said with a sigh. 'I'll have to wait for another to be dispatched.'

'No problem. I'll take you home,' Dr Harrison said, taking her arm and heading towards the car park. 'I could do with a drive to clear my head. The restaurant was a little stuffy.'

'That's very kind of you but I couldn't—'

'I insist,' he cut in. 'It's the least I can do to show my appreciation for your marathon first day on the job. Besides, there's really no point arguing, I always win. So where are you staying?'

After a quiet smile, she realised she was too tired to argue so gave him her address. His charm was indisputable and the ease with which he made Beth's pulse race gave her no reason to doubt he would always win. She looked down at his strong masculine hand holding her arm and the warmth of his skin made her spine tingle. She felt so good, so protected…and so close to exhaustion. Her tired eyes slowly climbed his body, daring to rest for a moment on his chiselled jaw and soft lips. At this close proximity, Beth guessed his body could be as commanding as his mind.

'Best be on our way,' he said with a voice more brotherly than seductive. She came down to earth with a crash. Dr Harrison was simply offering friendship to a new arrival in his city. And why would it be any different, she thought. She had seen his beautiful escort earlier in the evening. Still, being friends was more than she had expected from him this morning and it was infinitely better than being adversaries. Besides, she really didn't need a distraction or any complication and a man like Matthew would never fancy a woman like her, she decided. He would be looking for a worldly, gorgeous model type, definitely not a dishevelled, overtired resident clearly in need of a hot bath and a good sleep.

'Sounds fine to me,' she said, as they headed towards a dark-coloured BMW convertible. He opened her car door first and waited for her to get in before walking around to the driver's side and climbing in. Within minutes, Beth found that Dr Harrison hadn't bought the car for appearance alone.

After confirming the address of the one-bedroom maisonette the hospital exchange programme had found for Beth only fifteen minutes from the hospital, he took the car out on the main road and put his foot down hard on the accelerator. Beth's hand gripped the door handle tightly as her eyes found the speedometer. With the warm wind rushing by, she was glad her hair was still tied back in a plait, albeit wispy after almost fifteen hours on the job.

'Don't you worry we might be picked up for speeding?' she managed to say.

'I'm within the speed limit...maybe it just seems faster because you're tired,' he said, using one free hand to loosen his tie and undo the top button of his shirt.

Beth unsuccessfully fought the urge not to

stare at his appealing profile as she felt her heart start to pound. Everything in her mind was warning her not to look for trouble. He was so attractive and she felt sure he knew it. Somehow she had to keep her thoughts purely professional but he was making it difficult without a lot of effort.

His broad shoulders were relaxed against the leather seat, tanned skin revealed beneath his open shirt where his tie had been. How she wished the tie was back in place and the buttons were not open. She wondered how in her almost catatonic state she was mesmerised by his sensuality. This was ridiculous. It was like having a crush on a teacher. *Totally inappropriate*, she berated herself silently.

She mustered her thoughts. 'I was wondering why you were heading back to the hospital so late at night?'

'Some paperwork,' he answered flatly. Matthew had no intention of admitting that going home alone after dropping his sister back at her place was worse than the distraction of undertaking a few hours' paperwork at one in the morning. A good night's sleep had eluded him for years. Five years, to be exact.

Five long, lonely years since the accident.

The nights would turn into morning with just enough sleep to allow him to function. Anger, resentment and a lot of disappointment had taken his life and turned it into mere existence. He felt robbed of the happiness he had once enjoyed and had thought was to be his forever. He was nothing more than a shell of a man. An angry one at best, and at worst just empty and alone. But tonight this English woman, for some reason that he could not understand, was making him feel a little less angry and a little less empty.

'So what makes a young woman travel halfway around the world to do exactly what she could do in a London hospital?'

Beth thought better of blurting out her family issues and decided to go the pleasant route. 'I felt like a break from the cold English winters. Thought I'd swap wellies for sandals for a year or so.'

Matthew smiled. 'It does get cold here. You might need some socks to accompany your sandals around June and July.'

Beth smiled back at his response. She was very tired but enjoying the banter. Matthew was not just easy on the eye. He was amusing and put her at ease.

'I heard it doesn't snow here in Adelaide—is that right?'

'Yes, and to let you into a little-known secret...' Matthew looked away from the road and into Beth's eyes for a split second '...I've never seen snow.'

Beth was amused by his confession. But it was the nanosecond of his piercing blue eyes staring into hers that took her breath away. She had thought she was about to collapse from exhaustion when suddenly her body had come to life. She swallowed nervously. Matthew was making her feel alive in ways that even fully awake she hadn't felt before. She had to snap out of it. He was her boss and he was playing cab driver. *That's all*, she reminded herself. *You are not his type.*

'Really, you've never, ever seen snow?'

'No, never,' he conceded with a grin. 'My travel destinations are always the tropics up north. No chance of snow up there and there's none to speak of in Adelaide except maybe some muddy, icy fluff on the top of Mount Lofty, but you'd need a hunting party with magnifying glasses to find it.'

'Mount Lofty?'

'It's up that way.' He signalled with his hand to the foothills in the east. 'In a national park. Scenic enough, but there's definitely no ski resort up there.'

'Well, then, I did pack properly,' she announced. 'I left the wellies back home.'

Matthew suspected there was more to Beth's medical exchange than a desire to swap her footwear but since she was obviously close to exhaustion he decided not to ask more questions. He didn't need to know too much. He had to admit to himself that he found her cute, and feisty and a little mysterious. It was an intriguing package but it was also worrying. Matthew didn't want to be interested in Beth in any capacity other than as an exchange resident in his care. She would be there for twelve months and then she would be gone. Never to be seen again.

He put his foot down again as the lights changed to green, sending Beth's head back against the headrest. She was surprised to find they were nearing her street. It wasn't so much the conversation that had been riveting and had made fifteen minutes seem like five but the distracting speaker.

Beth released her seat belt and reached for the door handle. 'It's the next one on the left, number seven.'

'Do you roll out shoulder first from moving cars, or is it more of a hunched kind of a jump?' he asked with a smirk. Without waiting for her reply, he continued, 'Don't be in such a hurry to get out of the car, Dr Seymour.'

Indignant that she may have betrayed her desire to move away from him rather than the car, Beth was at least grateful the dim streetlights hid the heat she felt in her cheeks. From the corner of her eye she watched his mouth curve in the moonlight.

With impeccable manners, he jumped from the car, whisked around to Beth's side and opened her door. Quickly she climbed out and crossed the pavement to her gate. She didn't know what he was thinking and she prayed he didn't know what was on her mind. And the sooner she put distance between them, the better.

'I'll see you tomorrow, Dr Seymour,' he said, as he ran back to his side of the car.

'Thanks so much for the lift.' Feeling more relaxed with thirty feet between them, she added as she opened her front door, 'And please call me Beth when we're off duty.'

'You're welcome, Beth.' His voice was drowned by the noise of the engine as he took off down the street and into the night.

As Beth lay in bed that night she thought about the extraordinary day she'd had and more particularly the extraordinary Dr Harrison. He was nowhere near as bad as she had expected in some ways, and in other ways he was worse. He was an enigmatic man and working with him was going to be either hell or heaven, she could see it now. But for some strange, unfathomable reason she was looking forward to it. She had always enjoyed a challenge.

Tentatively she reached for the photograph of her family that stood on her bedside table. It had been taken in happy times. She smiled at the image of herself as a toddler, standing with her father, George, and mother, Grace. George, a surgeon, she knew would be impressed by the skill and dedication of a man such as Dr Harrison, and her mother, if she was still alive, would simply succumb to his charm.

She thought of the new additions to her family, those she left behind when she'd accepted her exchange to Australia, or, more accurately, those she had wanted to leave. There was no photograph. How she wished her life had been different.

When she'd been ten, and less than a year after her mother had passed away, her father had remarried and she'd gained a stepmother, Hattie, and a stepsister, Charlotte. Hattie was as warm as a refrigerated sardine and Charlotte, well, that had been an unhealthy competition from day one.

Beth rolled her sleepy eyes as the thought of Charlotte trying her best to pip her at every available opportunity to get George's attention. Unfortunately, with Hattie's assistance it had worked. After graduating from high school, Charlotte had decided against university and chosen to become a fitness instructor. Beth remembered the loud conversation that had occurred that night.

'Fitness instructor?' her father had questioned Hattie.

'And what may I ask is wrong with that?' she'd said with her eyes widening and, in Beth's opinion, becoming scarier by the minute.

'Nothing, absolutely nothing,' he'd replied, wishing he had never opened his mouth, but having done so he continued, 'It's a perfectly good career, but she's never shown an interest before. In fact, Charlotte has never had a gym membership to my knowledge. It seems a little out of the blue and I wonder if it isn't just a phase?'

'Don't be ridiculous, George,' Hattie had retorted. 'Charlotte has always wanted to be a personal trainer.'

The second storey of their home was immediately filled with every known piece of gym equipment but Charlotte failed to finish the course and dust began to settle on the large, expensive purchases. Pride wouldn't allow Hattie to admit George was right, so she climbed on the elliptical every second week for ten minutes and now and then lifted a two-pound weight and told everyone how marvellous she felt after her workout.

Charlotte decided to move into the retail sector, and with her perfect skin and stunning face she found employment with Dior in Harrods. After three weeks, and with enough skin-care purchases to open her own salon, she decided that standing all day was not her cup of tea, so she travelled abroad for two years, all paid for by her generous stepfather. George didn't question why she needed to travel first class and stay in five-star accommodation in order to 'find herself.' It wasn't worth the argument and days of silence that would follow. Hattie had set Charlotte's standards very high and George had grown accustomed to covering it all.

Finally, Charlotte returned from Paris and announced she was launching a career as an event planner. Beth felt enormously sorry for any poor brides who used her services for the entire planning process would no doubt centre around Charlotte and the brides would come in a poor second. Beth certainly knew how that felt.

Beth had tolerated Hattie and Charlotte but she was a little tired of hearing about Charlotte's accomplishments when her own top marks at school and later in medical school seemed to go unnoticed. When Beth graduated, she enjoyed a nice lunch with her father but that was it. There was no family celebration. She knew that Hattie was demanding and her father was trying his best to keep her happy by doing everything he could for his stepdaughter, but it hurt to be ignored.

She wanted a life where she wasn't last in line for pretty much everything. She didn't want expensive trips overseas, neither did she expect to be the child favoured by her father, but equal now and then would have been nice. It became unbearable the year after graduation. Charlotte was never happy, Hattie was always complaining and George was always busy trying desperately to appease them both. Beth had endured enough so she applied for a medical exchange to Australia.

In her heart, she knew her father had been proud of her over the years, and although he never said a lot around his new wife he often smiled and gave Beth an encouraging pat on her shoulder. The warm hugs she'd received him when she'd been a small child had disappeared when the ice queen had moved in. Beth had learnt to be her own best friend, and not expect any praise for her efforts, but it made her miss her mother even more.

Tucking the quilt up to her face, she snuggled in the warmth of her bed. She was happy to have a much-needed break from her stepfamily. Maybe the incorrigible Dr Harrison would be both a challenge and a distraction, she reflected. And maybe, given time, her father might even miss her.

Beth thought back to the timing of Matthew's apology. When she'd reacted badly to the addict, he could have berated her for allowing her emotions to come into play at work, reminding her of the need to remain detached, but he had chosen not to. Instead, he'd offered compassion and an apology. Beth suspected that hidden within the aloof Dr Harrison was a kind heart. He was obviously complicated, but that didn't faze Beth. He was also a complex man but so handsome and charismatic. In fact, lying in the warmth of her bed, Beth admitted to herself she was a little infatuated with him.

Then her practical nature reminded her

starry-eyed side that it was a little too soon to think about him in a romantic way. She still had a career to get on track and a relationship wasn't really in her plans. It hadn't ever been. The endless study hours she had put in to make the grade in medical school had ruined any chance of long-term romance. She had dated a fellow medical student in her second year but with the heavy study load and part-time jobs they'd both had, it had fizzled out after a few months. The times they had slept together had been awkward and the earth had never moved for Beth.

It hadn't been a heartbreaking decision to end it, as there had been no passion or real love. It had been a friendship that had crossed the line, and in hindsight they'd both admitted they were better as friends.

Beth had returned to her books, focused on being a doctor, and put love on hold. And now here she was, alone in the darkness of her room, entertaining the crazy idea of romance with a man as complicated as Dr Harrison. With his charisma and confidence she doubted there would be anything awkward about his bedside manner.

Beth smiled wickedly at that thought then plumped up her pillow and turned over once again. She drifted off to sleep wondering what punishment awaited Tom for leaving his little sister alone. It definitely wouldn't be pleasant when his parents finally caught up with him.

Morning came too quickly, bringing with it the shrill sound of the alarm. Wearily Beth climbed from bed, showered and prepared for her second day at the Memorial.

It wasn't by chance she chose to wear a slim navy skirt and soft wrap blouse of pale blue. She draped a soft cotton cardigan over her shoulders as the weather seemed slightly cooler than yesterday. Beth tried to convince herself that the extra attention to details had nothing to do with a certain A and E consultant. After all, she was very serious about her job and definitely not wanting to flirt.

Up until now she had always had an aversion to unpredictable men and equally she had never experienced any thrill in speed. But during her drive home last night, she'd found herself warming to both. And this morning she was surprised by the excitement she felt at the prospect of seeing Dr Harrison again. It was crazy and she knew it but there was something about the man that gave her butterflies. He had gone out of his way to take her home, and she wondered if there might have been more to it than just being polite. She liked the way he made her feel. He had asked her questions on the drive home and he had listened. She doubted it had been paying lip service, he'd seemed genuinely interested. But he was so handsome and she had seen his date.

As she sat in her sunroom enjoying her breakfast, reason was fighting her romantic thoughts when she suddenly spied the focus of her daydreams. Through the lace-draped window she watched Matthew striding purposefully up the garden path of her maisonette. Even more astonishing was the enormous bouquet of flowers in his arms.

She wiped her mouth with a napkin as her mind ran the gamut of emotions. *Control yourself, Beth*, she thought folding the napkin with shaking hands. *You're a grown woman, so show some degree of reserve. You have to play hard to get*, her pride reminded her, but all the while her heart raced as she thought anxiously about the possibility of Matthew Harrison having feelings for her. She had never thought it was possible to feel this way about a man so soon after meeting him. Beaming, she crossed to open the door just as he knocked.

'Good morning,' she greeted him.

'Lovely morning, isn't it?'

'Perfect,' she replied, trying to keep her eyes from blatantly admiring the gorgeous blooms.

'These are for you.'

'They're beautiful, but you shouldn't have,' she said as she took the flowers.

'I didn't,' he said, stepping back with a frown knitting his brow. 'The parents of the hit-and-run girl sent them to my office for you and I decided to bring them over. There's really no room for them in A and E,' he announced casually.

Beth was overcome with embarrassment. She wanted to fall between the cracks of the floorboards. She couldn't believe what she had said. Quickly she tried to cover her complete and utter humiliation. 'I meant you shouldn't have gone out of your way to bring them round. Now, if you'll excuse me, I'd better get ready for work.'

Beth couldn't believe for a split second she had actually thought that the head of A and E would bring her flowers. She had bought into her own daydreams. How stupid could she be? She had only started at the hospital the day before and after one kind gesture of driving her home she'd gone and stupidly thought her boss was interested. *Really, Beth,* she berated herself, *you have just made a complete fool of yourself.*

Realising Matthew must have seen through her pitiful cover-up, she turned away. She had to hide the mortification she knew would be written all over her face. She reached for the handle to close the door, but Matthew's leather-clad foot stopped her.

To be honest, Matthew didn't know why he had gone out of his way to deliver the flowers. There would have been somewhere to store them but something about this woman made him want to see her outside work. He hadn't felt this way in years and now he was close to her he was struggling with his feelings. It was unnerving and he decided quickly that he shouldn't be there. He couldn't afford to be there. He was relieved when his head took control over his heart and forced him to be brutal. He had been shut down emotionally for years and he had no intention of ever opening up.

'Listen, Beth, I think we should get something straight right here and now. I'm still not convinced about this whole exchange programme. If I have anything to do with it, you will be the last. There is nothing personal in this decision but if I had been successful with the board you would not have made it out here. I stopped the exchange programme at the Western Hills Hospital in Sydney a few years back and I intend to do the same here at Eastern.'

Beth opened her mouth to reply but was interrupted by the not-too-distant noise of screeching brakes, followed by the unmistakable and sickening sound of metal buckling and glass splintering.

'Looks like we've started work early this morning,' he said, heading down the path and looking in the direction of the accident. 'We can finish this talk later if I haven't made myself clear enough.'

Pushing her humiliation aside, Beth hurriedly reached for her keys and locked the front door while Matthew grabbed his mobile phone from the car. Together they ran down to the end of the street to where two cars had collided. It was a mess, with debris strewn all over the intersection and no sign of movement from within the compacted sedans. Beth feared the worst. Even though she had trained in A and E in London, and she had requested the same when she'd transferred, she still hadn't quite learnt to handle the feeling of dread in her stomach at times like this.

'I'll check the silver car. You do the blue,' he said as he raced to the car wedged between a lamp post and a large eucalyptus gum tree.

Beth looked both ways, and crossed the road to the blue hatchback. She peered inside to find the single occupant lying back against the driver's seat.

'What have you got over there, Beth?' she heard Matthew call out.

'Single female occupant, unconscious.'

'Ditto,' he called back. 'I'll call for two ambulances.'

Beth tugged at the driver's door in vain. In desperation she ran to the passenger side, to find it locked also. She tore off her cardigan and looked around on the ground for something hard. Half a discarded brick from a house under construction lay nearby. Reaching for it, Beth covered the window with the knitted top then smashed the glass. Thankfully it was an older model car with manual door locks so she reached inside carefully and unlocked the door.

The woman, who Beth guessed to be in her early twenties, was unconscious and bleeding profusely from a head wound. There was no time to be lost.

Sweeping away the broken glass from

the seat with her cardigan, Beth struggled with the restrictions of her tight skirt as she climbed across to find a pulse. Albeit faint, to her relief it was present and, as far as she could ascertain, regular. Untucking her own blouse, Beth used the hem to put pressure on the gash across the woman's forehead and continued at intervals to check her vital signs until the sirens of the ambulances became audible.

She wondered what Matthew had met with in the other car. As the paramedics neared the car she reached over and unlocked the driver's side door and undid the woman's seat belt.

'Suspected neck or spinal injures so we need a neck brace in place before the victim can be moved,' Beth informed the men. One paramedic retrieved a brace from the ambulance while the other released the woman's feet from the twisted pedals.

'Head injuries only?' he asked.

'As far as I can make out… Hell!' she cursed as she noticed the woman's skin become clammy and her pulse begin to race. She felt down to the woman's abdomen. It was now rigid.

'What's wrong?' the paramedic demanded.

'Where's the brace?' she called out, but it

was already on hand. Carefully she slipped it around the victim's neck. 'We may not have a lot of time. I suspect internal bleeding.'

Expeditiously the patient was lifted from the mangled vehicle and placed on the raised stretcher. Beth climbed from the car and raced over to the ambulance.

'I want her on oxygen, and saline IV.'

'I can travel with her to the Eastern,' came a low voice from behind them.

Beth turned around to see her solemn-faced consultant.

'Mine was not so lucky. She didn't make it.' He wiped his forehead with the back of his hand and took a deep breath. 'I've seen my share of death but it never gets any easier.'

'It makes you realise how precious life is. You should grab it with both hands,' Beth said solemnly.

Matthew looked at the woman standing before him. She could be forthright in her opinion, yet still vulnerable and caring. She was getting under his skin very quickly and that was causing him grief. But he didn't want to care about what she thought or felt. He just didn't want to care.

'We have one alive, so let's act on that,' he

said hurriedly as he climbed into the ambulance. 'What's the call here?'

'At best shock, head abrasions and possible neck injury. At worst, add internal bleeding.'

'Right, let's go. I'll take blood now for a cross-match and we can have her typed in half an hour. Call ahead and let them know I want O-neg ready in case of emergency,' he directed the paramedics, then reached into his pocket, pulled out his car keys and turned his attention back to Beth. 'Would you mind taking my car to the hospital?'

'No, but I haven't driven a manual shift for a long time,' she said as she watched him insert the IV line.

'Like riding a bike,' he said. 'But considering what I paid for that little imported job, please don't forget to change your clothes before you do.' Beth glanced down at her blood-stained blouse and skirt. It was going to be another day in slacks and a sensible cotton shirt, she mused.

In a wail of sirens the two ambulances took off into the traffic, leaving Beth with a prayer for the woman inside and the keys to a midnight-blue BMW that she hoped was well insured.

CHAPTER THREE

'You did it!' Beth congratulated herself as she pulled the car into the Eastern Memorial car park.

Despite thinking more than once that she had left the entire gearbox on the road during the shift from first to second, Beth managed to drive the expensive vehicle without a single incident. With a sigh of relief, she pulled the key from the ignition and took a deep breath.

Her mind raced back to the embarrassing start to the day. She hoped that Matthew would forget her ridiculous assumption that the flowers were from him. She also hoped the passenger had survived the trip to the hospital. It was touch and go with the woman's internal injuries but Beth was confident that a doctor as skilled as Matthew would give her the best chance of survival.

He was a complex man and, while respected and revered, he was definitely not loved by his staff. She wasn't sure why she was so attracted to him. Normally arrogant men left her cold, but there was something about Matthew that made her think that underneath his suit of armour was a different man. She felt in her heart that there was more to Matthew Harrison than met the eye, although that alone was pretty damned good. Her delicious thoughts were abruptly broken by the arrival of a mud-encrusted Range Rover in the parking bay opposite her. The huge grille in her line of vision was filled with splattered insect bodies. Goodbye, daydreams.

But what was she thinking anyway? Dr Harrison was dating a beautiful woman and had made it perfectly clear that morning that he didn't even want her at the hospital. Well, not her precisely but an exchange resident was definitely not on his wish list. Yet his body language the night before had stirred unexpected feelings in her. She smiled sheepishly at the driver of the Range Rover as she silently cringed at her irrational thoughts. She had never dated anyone like Matthew and doubted she would. She had already seen his standard, and a gorgeous blonde bombshell she definitely was not. Enough with the daydreaming, she thought as she grabbed her bag from the back seat and climbed out of the car.

Perhaps she should put the blame on jet-lag and a long first day at work. She wasn't herself at all. *Both pathetic excuses, Beth Seymour*, she chided herself.

The man was irrevocably under her skin, but since he made it painfully clear that he didn't feel the same way, she had to keep it to herself. He certainly shouldn't be held responsible for her romantic musing, so Beth decided quickly to curb her imagination by making sure she only saw Dr Harrison within the hospital grounds in future. No more lifts after work. She was far from home and feeling a little vulnerable, and now the poor unsuspecting Matthew Harrison was the focus of her attention. She had to keep everything in perspective. He was her boss. She was there to learn. Nothing more.

Hurriedly she locked the door, and feeling rather pleased that she had brought the car back safely she raced across the parking lot to the hospital entrance. She had changed into sensible beige slacks and a white cotton shirt and put her blood-stained clothes in her laundry tub to soak before she'd left home for the second time that day. As she made her way into A and E, she looked around for Matthew, hopeful of hearing good news about the car-accident victim. They had worked well together during the crisis that morning, and that was something she couldn't deny. But she mustn't make more of it than that.

She was still early, so she stopped to chat to Yvette in Reception for about five minutes, getting an update on the previous day's patients. Then she made a quick call to Paediatrics to check on Tania. She intended to visit her young patient as soon as she had a spare minute, to thank her personally for the beautiful flowers.

With no sign of Dr Harrison on the floor, she walked past his office and saw it was empty. Closing his door, she headed down to the doctors' lounge to see if he was there. She had to put her handbag in her locker anyway, she told herself. It wasn't as if she was going out of her way to find him.

'Morning, Beth,' came a cheerful voice from across the room.

'Good morning, Dan. You're in a very good mood. Any reason?' Beth asked as she adjusted her white consulting coat and took the hairbrush from her locker, all the while hiding her disappointment that it wasn't her consultant.

'Sir Harrison, the Almighty One, was civil

to me this morning. It was the first time he's greeted me with a "Good morning, Dan" in the six months I've been here.'

Beth crossed to the mirror with the brush in her hand. 'Do you know what happened with the RTA he brought in?'

'How did you hear about her?' Dan asked as he leant against the wall beside the mirror, staring at Beth with a curious look in his eyes.

'I was with him this morning when the accident happened,' she answered as she ran the brush through the unruly curls and then tied it all back with a thick black elastic band.

'Ah,' he said, rubbing his chin thoughtfully. 'So it's true what they're saying around here, then.'

'And what might that be?'

'That you and our beloved leader are more than good friends. News travels fast when doctors leave the hospital late at night together.' He moved towards her and playfully slipped his arm through hers. 'And may I say if his mood is a result of you, the Cas staff—no, the entire Eastern Memorial staff—should go down on our knees to you. You didn't waste any time, did you?'

'What a lot of rubbish,' she said, freeing

her arm from his and shaking her head. 'He drove me home, that's all.'

'And you were together this morning?' He grinned and nudged her in the ribs. 'Seems to me there's a few hours to account for, Dr Seymour! But I'm not one to pass judgment, especially when I benefit from your late-night efforts.'

'Don't be ridiculous. He came to my place with flowers this morning,' she said, rolling her eyes. 'He didn't stay the night!'

'Flowers? Not bad, Seymour,' he said with a smirk. 'I wait six months for a "Good morning, Dan", and you expect me to believe he gave you flowers just for the heck of it? Come on, you can do better than that.'

Realising that she was digging a deeper hole with every word, Beth decided to put an end to his insinuations. 'The flowers were from a patient and Dr Harrison simply delivered them to me.' Beth swallowed as she thought back to that embarrassing moment. The moment when she had prayed to be swallowed by the floorboards and never be seen again.

'Right. And floral deliveries to residents' homes are simply part of his job description.'

'He was just being friendly.'

'In case you didn't know, Harrison is rarely civil to residents, let alone friendly.'

Totally exasperated, Beth threw the brush in her locker and slammed the door closed. 'It was not a date!'

Running a finger across his mouth, Dan smiled. 'My lips are sealed...your secret is safe with me.'

'Oh, you're being ridiculous!' she retorted as she left the room. 'I'll go and find out how the RTA is going myself.'

'No need,' came Dr Harrison's voice. 'She's in Theatre now. You were right with your suspicions about the internal bleeding. She'd ruptured her spleen.'

Beth was mortified when she realised that Dr Harrison had been standing there during her exchange with Dan. How much had he heard? she wondered as the heat rose in her cheeks. Biting her lip nervously, she turned round. 'How does it look for her?'

'Pretty good, I'd say, but that's not why I'm here.' The glare of his eyes didn't move from hers as he folded his arms defensively. 'Have you got something to tell me, Dr Seymour?'

Beth swallowed hard. By the look on his face, it was clear that he must have overheard at least part of their conversation. As his frown deepened and his jaw tensed further,

she guessed it was probably Dan's allusion
to romance. She prayed he didn't believe that
she was intimating to Dan there had been
more to the drive home. After the flower incident, and now this, she felt sure his opinion of her would fall even further. If that was
possible.

'About what, Dr Harrison?' she asked, trying not to appear as uncomfortable as she
was feeling at that moment. She wanted to
wring Dan's neck.

'About my car.'

'Oh, that.' She let out her breath. She was
so happy he was not bringing up her morning faux pas, and particularly not in front of
Dan. She wanted to keep a shred of dignity
with her co-worker at least. 'It was a piece of
cake, no need to thank me. In fact, I'll do it
again any time. I had a wonderful time when
I got over my initial nerves.'

'Had a wonderful time. Are you completely mad?' The volume and tone of his
voice sent Dan scurrying out of the room and
down the corridor for cover.

Beth looked quizzical. 'What on earth are
you talking about? You asked me to bring the
car back and I did just that.'

'I mistakenly thought you might have been
honest with me, Dr Seymour.' His anger was

equally directed at himself for expecting more from a woman. He had gone against his better judgement and had hoped she would have had the integrity to stand up to her mistake and take responsibility. But she had run away. Before this she had made him want to believe she was trustworthy. *As if any woman could be trustworthy!* He berated himself to think for a moment that any woman could be honest. No, he knew women who got close to him seemed to have the ability to run away from responsibility—and from him.

'What are you talking about?' she demanded in an equally raised voice.

'My almost written-off car.'

'I left the car in perfect order in the car park. You must be looking at the wrong car.'

'I wish I was, but unfortunately I just retrieved my case notes and diary from the back seat of the wreck,' he answered, shaking the notes and diary in his tightly clenched hand.

'But I had nothing to do with it, I swear.'

'I thought you would at least have the integrity to admit to it.' He scowled as he paced the room.

'But I'm telling you,' Beth cut in, 'I returned your car in perfect condition.'

'I'd always rated punctuality as an important trait amongst my residents. Perhaps I should rethink my priorities and put honesty above it on the list of prerequisites. That would find you struck off this hospital's personnel list.'

'This is unbelievable. I did you a favour, under duress, I might add, and this is what I get in return?' she spat, ignoring his seniority momentarily. She couldn't believe she had ever found this ogre of a man attractive. And she certainly didn't care at this moment what he thought of her. 'I wish you had driven the stupid car yourself!'

'Well that makes two of us!'

'Ahem,' came a voice from behind the warring pair.

'Yes,' Dr Harrison yelled at the orderly. 'What do you want?'

'The gate attendant told me to give you this.' The orderly nervously handed over a slip of paper and prepared to leave.

'Not so fast,' Dr Harrison bellowed. 'What is this?'

'The registration number of the four-wheel drive that cleaned up your car before it reversed from the parking lot. He said it made off without stopping.'

'Maybe trust should be a prerequisite of A and E consultants!' Beth retorted as she stormed off, seething, her head held high in bittersweet victory. No one would ever again speak to her with such little respect. She had given her word and he had called her a liar!

She disappeared from view before giving a suddenly humbled Dr Harrison a chance to respond, and rounded the corner into the waiting room, still visibly fuming.

'Well, that puts paid to me asking for tomorrow off,' said Dan as he finished writing up the last patient's notes. 'Thought I'd try my luck, until Romeo blew you away.'

'He's not my Romeo, Dan, please just leave it alone.'

'Not now anyway, but maybe if you make him supper at your place and—'

'Dan!' she cut in with a chill in her voice to let him know she had endured about as much as she intended. She was so disappointed that Matthew had pronounced her guilty without any proof.

'Well, you somehow made him the closest thing to human since I got here, even if it was for only five minutes.' Dan reached for the next patient's file, and began reading the nurse's notes.

'Why is he so quick to find the worst in everyone?' Beth asked, anger still colouring her voice.

'Not completely sure,' Dan began, lifting his eyes from the file and then checking around quickly that the focus of their conversation was not in sight. 'He's been a right royal pain since he arrived here three years ago, I was told. I was filled in quickly when I started. No one really knows the whole story but there was something about a car accident a few years ago, and a broken engagement. Not sure how it all fits together but it apparently changed him from Jekyll into Edward Hyde. That all happened in Sydney and then he transferred here—'

'Single gunshot wound,' Yvette interrupted the conversation. 'ETA five minutes.'

'I'll take it,' Dan said, raising his eyebrows at the admissions nurse. 'Bay two okay?'

'I'll help,' Beth said, as she watched Yvette check the whiteboard and nod.

'Not on this one,' he began. Leaning across the desk, he turned his attention back to Yvette. 'Call for Dr Mulloway, the surgical consultant. He'd want to be here, and get a crash trolley in room two now.'

Beth stepped aside graciously. 'You know where I am.'

It was only a few minutes before the paramedics rushed the barouche through the entrance. Beth shuddered to see it was a child victim, no more than five, she guessed, with a wound to the face. The bandage around his head and the clothes of his upper torso were heavily stained with blood, and an oxygen mask was being held in place over the bloodied mess by the paramedic. A distraught woman raced in behind, trying to cling to the child's arm.

'He's my baby,' the mother cried as Yvette rushed to her. 'You don't understand, he's all we've got. You have to save him.'

'Dr Berketta will do everything he can,' the nurse reassured her. 'But he won't be able to if you get in the way.'

'But he needs me. Oh, dear God, I don't know how he found the gun. My husband always locks it away when he gets home from work. He's a security guard.'

Yvette put her arm around the woman then, catching Beth's attention, signalled with her eyes towards the empty reception desk and a look of *help me out*. 'We can go in with your son, but we must stay back and let the doctors do their work.'

Beth nodded, and was happy to step in until Vivian or another nurse returned to Reception. She made her way behind the desk as Yvette rushed the woman to bay two.

Beth couldn't help but notice Dr Harrison's

absence in A and E all morning. Not that she minded. She was still fuming at how easily he assumed the worst of her. She wanted an apology that he apparently wasn't prepared to offer. Although from all accounts, including Dr Harrison's own admission, she had already received one from him, which was more than any of her peers had ever received. Perhaps if they were in her position that honour would be reward enough in itself. But for Beth it wasn't. She needed to know that her word was enough.

Despite her anger at the incident, Beth was curious as to what could possibly have happened to make Matthew so distrusting of those around him. So quick to think the worst of them. He was moody, yet she had also witnessed his caring side with patients and his sense of humour on the drive home. He could be so easy to talk to and yet so short at times.

But why did she even care what made him tick? She didn't need more problems in her life. She had changed continents for a reason.

It was shortly before one when Dan suggested she take a lunch break. The child with the gunshot wound had been stabilised, but they were still waiting for the craniofacial specialist from the Central Children's Hospital to arrive and assess him for transfer.

Apart from a minor abrasion, a rusty nail through a shoe, which had required a tetanus booster, and a case of measles that Beth had referred back to a general practitioner, the morning had been quiet, with the noticeable absence of Attila.

She was incensed every time she thought of his accusation.

Finally, against her better judgement, she asked Yvette, 'Where is Dr Harrison? He hasn't been in all morning.'

'He's been in a meeting on six. Apparently some bigwig consultant is arriving here tomorrow from England and everyone's been put on their toes. Just our hospital director, Dr Lancaster, having his usual panic.'

Beth was confused about why she cared where Matthew was and what he might be doing. She wondered what masochistic gene was driving her to ask. She apparently didn't understand her emotions very well at the moment but she did know she was hungry. Thinking better of a vending-machine lunch, Beth headed for the lifts and the fourth-floor cafeteria. As she passed A and E bay five she spied Matthew down on his knees, strapping an ankle. She pretended she hadn't seen him and continued on her way. But she had gone only a few steps when his voice echoed along the corridor.

'Dr Seymour, may I have a word with you?'

Beth looked over her shoulder to see him tug anxiously on his stethoscope for a moment before slipping it from around his neck and putting it into his pocket. He took long, purposeful strides down the corridor towards her.

'Is this about work?' she countered briskly, trying her hardest not to be affected by his nearness.

'Beth.' He paused to take a breath. 'This is ridiculous.'

Her eyes widened. 'I think it would be better if you addressed me as Dr Seymour from now on, and in return I will give you the same courtesy.'

'We have to clarify things.'

'As far as I'm concerned, there's absolutely nothing else to clarify about this morning. Your opinion of me is crystal clear.'

With that she continued on her way, praising herself quietly for not allowing her desires to colour her judgement. She wasn't about to let him clarify anything. It had to be an outright apology, nothing else would do.

No man would ever walk all over Beth Seymour, whatever his position. She was worth more than that. Her time of being treated like her feelings didn't matter was over. She hadn't moved ten thousand miles to make the same mistakes and accept less than she deserved.

Sitting in the noisy cafeteria, Beth was halfway through her chicken salad when she noticed a tall figure hovering over her table.

'I did ask you politely to leave me alone,' she declared, without giving him the courtesy of raising her eyes.

'An English woman with a bit of fight. Glad we haven't turned you into a shrinking violet. Aussies can do that if you let them. Bit overbearing we are at times,' said the middle-aged man with a wink that went unnoticed by Beth.

Her agitated state and the realisation she had just offended some innocent man caused Beth to swallow a large piece of chicken that had not been chewed properly. The pain of it travelling down her oesophagus made her wince and her eyes started to water. She tried not to show her pain as she gulped water, hoping it would aid the passage of the chicken down her throat.

'Are you all right, Dr Seymour?' asked the

concerned stranger in a worried tone as he pulled up a chair and sat down next to Beth.

The lump of chicken had made its way slowly to the point where Beth was finally able to swallow it and the pain subsided. Wiping the tears from the corners of her eyes, Beth feigned a smile. 'Yes…I'm quite fine, thank you.'

'I apologise for startling you. Looks like I made something go down the wrong way.'

'Honestly, I am all right. I feel a bit silly, actually.'

'Please don't, totally my fault,' the man began, as he put out his hand. 'But I must introduce myself. I'm the hospital director, Edward Lancaster.'

Beth met his handshake, all the while thinking she had probably ended her career by offending this man. With a nervous sigh she replied, 'Pleased to meet you. I'm Beth Seymour.'

'Yes, I know who you are, Dr Seymour. I came here looking for you. I have a favour to ask.'

A puzzled frown came to Beth's normally smooth brow. She wondered how she could possibly assist the hospital director. Perhaps her parking skills were now hospital news and he had a Mercedes or a Rolls Royce she could park somewhere to be written off for an insurance claim.

'What is it I can do for you?'

'I like that attitude, Dr Seymour. Positive. You'll do well with that approach, I can feel it already.'

Beth smiled back a little nervously.

'You may have heard we are going to have the pleasure of Professor Rowe's presence in the hospital for three months. He's arriving tomorrow and I was wondering if you would be available for a welcoming dinner at my home tomorrow evening.'

'I would be honoured. But why me? I'm only a resident.'

'Ah, but you're both new arrivals from England, and I thought Professor Rowe might find it comforting to hear a familiar accent among the flood of Australian drawls.' He reached into his pocket and pulled out a gold-edged card. 'I've taken the liberty of cutting your shift short tomorrow, as a bit of an incentive for you to accept. If you do, it will ensure you can make it by seven. The details are on here. Dress is formal.'

Beth had no choice, but the thought of a short shift was definitely an incentive. And the reality was she was going to dinner, whether she liked it or not. There was no way she would refuse an invitation from the director of the hospital.

'I'll see you tomorrow evening, Dr Seymour.'

'I'm looking forward to it,' she replied politely, despite being not entirely sure how she felt.

'Oh, by the way, Dr Seymour,' he added as he rose from the table and pushed in his chair, 'I have taken the liberty of arranging for Dr Harrison to be your dinner partner. I hope you don't mind. It was actually my wife's idea. She thinks he's rather charming. Can't see it myself but I have learnt over the years not to argue with Dorothy. Ever!'

'And what does Dr Harrison think about the prospect of being saddled with me?' Beth retorted.

'From the way he reacted when I mentioned my proposal a few minutes ago, he was anything but upset with the idea,' he replied as he tapped the top of the chair and left.

Beth watched his lanky frame cross the cafeteria floor and cordially acknowledge a number of staff on the way out. His words ran through her mind. Dr Harrison was anything but upset. But how did she feel?

Confused, she lamented. Terribly confused. The short time she spent with Matthew had her running a gamut of emotions.

It was almost five o'clock before Beth ran into Matthew by the lifts. Her day had been steady and between patients her mind had been preoccupied with thoughts of her dinner escort for the following evening.

'Dr Seymour.'

Beth stepped back as she met his cool blue stare. He was uncomfortably close to her. She felt her pulse quicken and her heart pound as she focused on his masculine features, particularly the firmly moulded mouth that lingered so close to hers. 'Yes, Dr Harrison?'

'I just wanted…well, I think perhaps I owe you…' His jaw flicked spasmodically as he faltered. 'What I'm trying to say is…'

Beth didn't offer any prompting. She intended to enjoy his discomfort. It would surely be one of the rare occasions Matthew was lost for words.

'Well, you know what I mean.'

'No, I'm afraid I don't.'

'You're determined to make this difficult, aren't you?'

Beth just stared in silence. His level of disquiet was almost palpable, but all good things had to end, she decided as she chose to conclude his suffering. 'Are you trying to say you're sorry?'

'Yes. I'm sorry,' he said, as if he was relieved to have the words pass over his lips. 'Very sorry about this morning. I jumped to the wrong conclusion. It's a bad habit of mine.'

Beth watched as he rubbed the back of his neck agitatedly.

'We're all human,' she said softly, 'and I accept your apology.'

'Thank you,' he answered huskily.

Suddenly she found her limbs strangely weak as he moved closer. She didn't move away. The husky tone of his voice made her tremble. She wanted to run but instead she allowed him to draw her near. His lean arm wrapped tightly around her shoulder and she felt his eyes resting on her lips. She felt her breath being stolen by the sweetness of his embrace.

Suddenly Matthew felt the need to pull away. He felt the warmth of Beth close to him and he didn't want to feel that level of comfort or intimacy. It felt strangely secure, and Matthew didn't believe in that feeling. He didn't trust it. And knew it didn't last.

'Perhaps this resident exchange will work

well after all,' he announced as he dropped his arm and, with a safe distance between them, walked in the direction of A and E.

Beth took a few minutes to calm the raging desire that Matthew had stirred in her. She ought to have learned her lesson by now, she realised as she fell into step beside him.

There was something that prevented this man showing his feelings. But what? she wondered. Certainly not a fear of rejection, because he would have to be blind not to know the effect he was having on her. But for his own reasons he clearly didn't want to reciprocate any romantic feelings. Perhaps it was their working relationship. He may have thought it was inappropriate as he was her superior. Or it may have been that he just didn't find her attractive. Looking down, she spied her dull beige slacks and shapeless consulting coat, and from the corners of her eyes she noticed stray wisps of her unruly hair. How could he find her attractive? She didn't belong in the same universe as the vision in the stunning red evening dress.

Feeling horribly self-conscious, she looked at her watch. 'It looks like I've almost finished for the day,' she announced, exceedingly grateful that she had an excuse to get away from him. As an afterthought she added, 'I'll see you in the morning.'

'I'm speaking at a conference tomorrow, but I'll be back for dinner tomorrow night. Apparently we're dinner partners.'

'So I heard,' she replied, trying very hard to sound as detached as possible. 'If you'd rather take your friend, I would understand.'

'You mean last night's date?'

'Yes,' Beth answered quietly. 'It really is fine with me. I don't need an escort, I'm sure.'

'That wasn't a date. That was my sister, Sylva. She graduated with her music degree and we went out to celebrate. It was a lovely evening and I'm very proud of her because I can't play a musical instrument to save my life. But getting back to the subject of dinner tomorrow night, I'm looking forward to a night off from here.'

Sister? Of course she was his sister, she was gorgeous. They had both benefited from the same spectacular gene pool.

But you're quite bright, she tried to reassure herself, and some men even like mad, curly hair.

'I'm sure it will be an interesting evening,' she replied under her breath as she nodded goodbye to the night-shift nurses. She was

trying to find a way to take her mind off Dr
Harrison. Trying to dismiss the way he was
making her heart pound so fast and her skin
tingle.

It was a good try but it didn't work.

She turned back to her A and E consultant,
giving him a half-hearted smile. 'I'll see you
there, then.'

'I thought I'd pick you up about seven.'

Every word he said made it harder for her
to forget the thrill of his body close to hers.
She didn't trust herself in the confines of his
fast car. She didn't want to make a fool of
herself again. He clearly didn't feel the same
way, so it was self-inflicted torture to spend
unnecessary time with him. At least until the
flower episode was a faint memory.

'If you don't mind, I'd find it easier to
make my own way there.'

He stood staring at her for a moment, not
uttering a word. Her heart began to race as
she wondered what was on his mind. Could
he see through her fragile charade?

'If that's what you would prefer, so be it.'
Plunging his hands into the depths of his
white duty coat pockets, he smiled and put a
welcome distance between them.

Welcome to both of them.

That was much easier than Beth had

thought it would be…until Matthew called across the hallway, 'I know for a fact that you don't have a car, so I'll drive you home after dinner tomorrow.'

Beth held that uncomfortable thought for the rest of the evening and all through her restless night.

When she arrived home she wanted to try on the dress she had bought for her medical graduation dinner and had brought out from England with her, but she was too exhausted to bother. Instead, she set the alarm to wake her half an hour earlier in the morning to give her time before work to check if it still looked all right to wear to dinner at Dr Lancaster's house.

She sat on the end of her bed and gently pulled her hair free from the elastic, her mind on Matthew all the while. As the spiral curls fell about her shoulders she pictured him running his hands lightly through her hair and tenderly caressing her face. She slipped into bed wishing there was a chance he was thinking about her at this moment. Could Dan be right? Was Matthew treating her differently from the other residents he had trained? She genuinely doubted it, but it was a lovely thought.

She reached over for her lamp and turned

it off, darkening the room. As she looked up towards the ceiling, she pictured her handsome boss. Was he sleeping peacefully in his bed or working late again? She turned to face the wall and closed her eyes, trying to block out thoughts of him. This was going to be a long night.

Looking in the mirror at the deep green satin evening gown in the early morning light, she wondered if it wasn't too revealing. She'd had her doubts when she'd bought it, but the salesgirl had reassured her that it complemented the chestnut tone of her hair. It did feel good, but the low-cut cowl neckline and even lower back with shoestring straps and figure-hugging floor-length skirt wasn't her usual style.

It had been a rebellious purchase. As there had been no real family celebration of her finishing her medical studies, she had decided to let her hair down and wear something completely out of character. She had felt sure that for once the family would notice her when the limousine turned up and she waltzed down the stairs in her slinky dress. But to her dismay, they had all been out at one of Hattie's fundraisers and she'd had no grand exit. No one to tell her that she looked even a little bit pretty.

She had locked the door of the empty house when she'd left that night and had decided she wouldn't be overlooked any more. She was going to make changes in her life. The first would be applying for an exchange to the furthest country from home. Australia.

Beth smiled to herself. She had done it and now here she was in the same dress on the other side of the world, and with the prospect of a most handsome dinner partner.

Beth felt a little concerned as she stepped back to scrutinise herself in the mirror. But then, with a mischievous grin in her eyes, she thought perhaps a dress like this would make a certain A and E consultant sit up and take notice, and that might not be such a bad thing after all. He was bringing out a side of her she had never thought existed. He was giving her attention, even though it was on a friendly rather than romantic level. Beth liked it. It had been a long time since anyone had noticed her. With the arrival of her stepfamily she'd been lost in the fuss they made about themselves. It had been easier to just blend into the background. But tonight would be different. Maybe if the stars aligned, she could shift his attention from friendly to something more.

The dress was perfect, but the dark circles under her eyes from lack of sleep were another matter. She would have to conceal them with make-up. She slipped out of the dress, carefully leaving it lying across her bed, while she searched for her pearl choker and earrings. On the long flight out she had kept her jewellery with her in her carry-on rather than in her checked-in luggage in case any suitcases went astray.

She found the precious pieces and placed them on her dressing table. They had belonged to her mother and she was so happy to have them. They made her feel special, just as her mother had made her feel as a little girl. Like she was the centre of her mother's universe. Just holding them in her hand brought back that feeling of belonging. One day she hoped to give them to a daughter of her own. To make that little girl feel as loved and as protected as she had once felt. Beth smiled at the thought of having a child. She wondered if Matthew had any children, or whether he wanted to have them.

You've completely lost your marbles, Beth Seymour, she said to herself. Shaking her head, she grabbed her underwear from the drawer and headed in for her shower. *It must be the Australian sun*, she mused as she turned on the piping-hot water.

CHAPTER FOUR

BETH WAS GRATEFUL her day was a short one. Dr Lancaster had arranged with Matthew for her shift to end at twelve-thirty, as he had mentioned the previous day. The morning in A and E had been busy and Beth had dealt with a multitude of patients, including a high-profile netballer with a sprained ankle, an elderly patient transported in from a nearby nursing home after a stroke, a middle-aged man with acute symptoms of a duodenal ulcer, and a young man in respiratory failure linked to his HIV status who was immediately transferred to ICU.

Beth was relieved to hand over to Dan and head home to prepare for the evening. Although the patient load had been unrelenting and her focus had been on ensuring they all received the highest medical care, in the moments between patients her thoughts had wandered to her enigmatic dinner partner and the thought of their drive home together. She had never felt so confused. Matthew had got under her skin in the way no man ever had. He was a mystery to Beth. So strong and caring but, in the same breath, so distant.

The entire situation was ridiculous. She had known Matthew for only two days—two emotionally torturous days—and he was on her mind constantly.

He seemed to be keeping her at a distance and then, without warning, pulling her close and causing her to imagine he had feelings for her. And those feelings seemed so real. She was not sure if she was reading too much into the brief time they'd spent together.

Was he genuinely interested in her as a woman or just as a friend? Was he even aware of what he was doing and how he was making her feel? Beth was not sure what to make of the man. He was a great doctor— she had witnessed that first-hand. There must be a reason for his difficult manner. Perhaps it had something to do with the accident or the broken engagement, or perhaps both. She wanted to ask about his past but she felt the timing had to be right. Maybe with a man like Matthew there would never be a right time.

'Off to dinner at Lancaster's, then?' Dan

asked, after taking notes on the morning's patients and their updated statuses.

Beth just stared blankly in silence at Dan. She was so deep in thought his remark went unanswered.

'Earth to Beth…' Dan said light-heartedly. 'I asked if you're hobnobbing with the board tonight?'

Beth realised after handover her thoughts had quickly moved a million miles away. 'Oh, yes, Dr Lancaster invited me to dinner yesterday.'

'Nice, very nice,' he answered playfully. 'You are definitely the fastest-moving resident ever. Flowers from the A and E consultant yesterday and dinner with the hospital director tonight, and it's only day three. I expect a hospital wing named after you by month-end!'

'Very funny, Dan,' she said. 'Apparently there's a visiting professor from the UK at the hospital and Dr Lancaster thought he might like to hear an English accent at dinner tonight.'

'Not judging here, Beth, you've got that whole sweet and innocent thing going on but, girl, you sure know how to work it.' Dan winked at Beth then gathered his notes and headed for the door. 'Oh, by the way, will Attila be attending?'

Beth dreaded admitting she was his date but knew it would get back eventually. 'Dr Harrison is my date for the evening.'

Dan went down on one knee with his arm raised and his fist clenched in victory. 'Awesome, absolutely awesome.' Then, climbing back to his feet, he added, 'We should all have a great day tomorrow if you just play nicely with him.'

'You're despicable, Dan,' Beth spat in an equally playful tone, despite being unnerved by the entire situation.

She wasn't sure what the evening would bring. Part of her was excited and the other part nervous, very nervous. Was she trying to rush things? Should she hold back? She wasn't sure how she felt.

Dan closed the door to the doctors' lounge behind him, leaving Beth with her thoughts. She shook her head in disbelief at her predicament. She had feelings far too soon for a man who was completely unfathomable. Beth opened the door to the adjoining room, crossed to her locker and placed her white coat and stethoscope inside. She removed her handbag and some exquisite chocolate champagne truffles that Yvette had been sweet enough to pick up for Beth to give to her dinner hosts. Beth carefully placed the gold and white wrapped box in her bag, before closing her locker again. Tonight would and could be many things but Beth knew dull would definitely not be one of them.

The green satin dress was definitely a statement, Beth decided as she checked her image in the mirror. She had straightened her hair and twisted it into a chic French roll, securing it with a simple clasp, and finished her outfit with her mother's pearl choker and earrings. She brought her hand to her throat and gently touched the precious necklace. Although the pearls were cool to the touch there was warmth and love radiating from them. Beth knew her mother would be happy if she could see her tonight.

Her shoes were silver slingbacks with a kitten heel. She had bought them for her graduation celebration and, knowing she would be standing for quite a while during the cocktail party, she'd chosen a height that was elegant but not uncomfortable. Her make-up was simple but a little heavier than the way she applied it during the day. Her eyes were smoky and her lips were a subtle matte red. Carefully applied perfume was the final touch.

She spied the cab arrive through the window. This would be the easiest part of the evening, she thought as she grabbed her clutch purse and made her way out of the house. The trip to Edward and Dorothy Lancaster's home in Hazelwood Park, a leafy eastern suburb of Adelaide, took about twenty minutes.

With a sigh hovering on her lips, she lifted the hem of her gown and carefully made her way through the paved archway of scented jasmine. A single cricket could be heard above the gentle spray of the garden sprinklers.

She made her way up the white stone steps to the front door of the Tudor-style home. She hesitated for a moment on the last step, turning to watch the cab leaving the sweeping grounds. A gravel driveway lined with delicate pastel roses in full bloom divided the expanse of manicured lawn and a high brush fence surrounded the grounds.

The sun was setting on the warm evening. Lights softly illuminated the enormous gumtrees, casting long shadows across the lawn, while delicate scents filled the air.

On another night Beth would truly have appreciated the beauty.

She rang the door chime and waited nervously. But the wait was short-lived agony as the door opened to a jovial Dr Lancaster.

'Good evening, Beth. I'm so glad you were able to be here,' he greeted her warmly, before stepping aside. 'Do come in.'

Beth swallowed the lump in her tense throat. She was very aware she was in the home of the hospital director. 'Thank you, Dr Lancaster, I'm very honoured to have been asked.'

Her congenial host insisted she call him Edward and then directed her to the patio where the dinner was to be held.

'You must be Dr Seymour,' a beautifully dressed older woman said with her hand outstretched. 'I'm Dorothy Lancaster.'

'I'm pleased to meet you, Mrs Lancaster,' Beth returned. 'And these are for you,' she added as she gave the beautifully wrapped box of truffles to her hostess.

'Thank you, dear. I will leave you to mingle with the young ones. Aperitifs are being served now and dinner will be served in about half an hour.' Dorothy smiled and headed back inside with the sweat treats.

Matthew wasn't in sight and part of Beth

secretly hoped that he wouldn't show at all. Her emotions were at odds and despite the time she had taken to get ready, she wasn't sure what message she wanted to send to her boss or how to react to him.

'Now, that is a dress a man could never forget.'

Beth didn't need to turn around to know who had muttered those words. The husky voice that was quickly sending shivers down her spine belonged to none other than Matthew. It was distinctive, deep and naturally sexy. There was nothing forced or put on in it. This man just had a voice as smooth as liquid chocolate. A voice that made Beth entertain very bad thoughts. A voice that she wanted to hear in the middle of the night… She had to snap out of it.

'Matthew,' Beth said as she turned to face her tormentor. 'Lovely to see you.' She hoped her casual, friendly tone would mask the desire he had once again stirred in her. The warm evening breeze was moving the draped back of her dress against her bare skin and making her very aware she had little covering her body. The last time she'd worn this dress she hadn't had any of these feelings. It wasn't the dress making her feel this way, it was definitely the man next to her. He was making her feel more of a woman than she had ever felt. And he wasn't even touching her.

Matthew looked at Beth and wondered if she knew how that dress was affecting him. He had thought over the last two days that she was very pretty in a girl-next-door kind of way, with her crazy auburn curls framing her sweet face and her big brown eyes. But tonight he was finding it hard to ignore the fact that she was a very desirable woman. Until now her figure had been hidden under a shapeless white consulting coat.

He had tried to keep his attention purely professional but as she stood before him tonight his eyes roamed her body and eagerly returned to the naked curve of her back. Emotions he'd thought dead and buried were suddenly very much alive. He wasn't sure he liked feeling this way again but he had no control. Beth was making his ability to think logically very difficult. His desire to keep his distance from her was fighting his desire for her. This was going to be a tough evening for him and he knew it would take every ounce of his self-control not to sweep this woman into his arms and make love to her…or at the very least kiss her.

'So, have you met our guest of honour?'

Matthew said abruptly, breaking the spell under which they were both unwillingly falling.

'No,' she replied. 'Have you?'

Gently linking Beth's arm through his, Matthew escorted her in the direction of the balcony, 'Not yet, but I suspect he will seek you out and we will both meet him. I understand you were seconded here tonight to make him feel at home.'

Beth smiled and nodded as she gently released her arm from Matthew's. If he was capable of stirring these longings with an innocent touch, in a crowded situation, she hardly dared to think what passion she would feel alone with him. Being this close to Matthew and having her feelings in upheaval made it difficult for Beth to verbalise much that sounded intelligent at this moment, so she just admired the view of the Adelaide foothills without saying a word. It was a perfect summer evening and she was soaking up the elegant yet relaxed ambience of her surroundings.

She wanted so much for Matthew to put his arm around her and pull her close, but she knew that wouldn't happen so she kept things purely professional and friendly, like two work associates at dinner. Because that was exactly what they were, she reminded herself. He had made that very clear.

Matthew fought the urge to put his arm around Beth. He feared he was fighting a losing battle against his need to be close to this woman. She had passion and dedication to her work that he had observed over the last few days, and a feisty nature that he admired. Beth looked so fragile and delicate yet underneath was a strong, determined woman. She was a walking contradiction and like no other woman he had ever met. She stood up to him without thinking about the consequences. She was passionate about her work and wouldn't tolerate his rants. She made him want to apologise for his poor behaviour.

For the last five years he had very easily controlled his emotions. Work had been his mistress. He had completely immersed himself in his role at the hospital. He worked late and took on extra duties that kept him from having the time to want or need a love life. His heart had been turned to rock after his fiancée had left him just when he'd needed her most. He looked down at his legs and knew that underneath the sharp creases in the Italian fabric were the fading scars of the accident. While they were hardly noticeable now, he doubted that the scars deep inside him would ever disappear.

Matthew knew he could not survive another heartbreak like the last one. He refused to let that happen. He needed distance so he could come to his senses. And he needed it quickly.

'I think I'll find us a drink,' he said abruptly. 'What would you like?'

'A red wine would be lovely.'

Beth watched as Matthew turned in silence and walked across the balcony to the bar, leaving her standing alone. His tall silhouette was commanding as he took long, purposeful strides across the decking. His black dinner suit highlighted his broad shoulders and his black hair was slicked back in waves ending at the tanned skin of his neck. She watched as the bartender gave him the drinks and he quickly raised a wine glass to his parted lips like a man dying of thirst. How she longed to feel those lips pressed against hers. They were wasted on the cold, thin rim of crystal.

She quickly turned away. The last thing she wanted was for Matthew to catch her watching him. She tried to focus on the view of the towering gum trees lining the narrow meandering creek in the distance, although the beautiful scenery was completely lost on her. Nature had no chance of competing with the vision in the dinner suit.

Dinner was quite delicious; a starter of leek and asparagus soup, a main of grilled quail and sautéed vegetables and the dessert was a raspberry and peach trifle with dark chocolate shavings.

Beth found Professor Rowe, the visiting dignitary, to be a charming man with a wonderful sense of humour. She discovered that he had once worked with Beth's father in London when they had both been surgical residents many years before. The world was indeed small and conversation flowed easily between them. Matthew appeared a little distracted all evening and he didn't participate in the conversation very much but Beth noticed him watching her at times. It didn't make her feel uncomfortable just the opposite, in fact, but as their eyes met he looked away. She wondered what was on his mind, but thought better of asking him. And she certainly wasn't about to share what she was thinking.

The time flew by and the evening drew to a close. Beth said goodnight to Professor Rowe, and thanked Edward and Dorothy Lancaster for their wonderful hospitality. She looked for Matthew and spied him at the bar, speaking with a group of consultants from the hospital. Although she had been nervous about the trip home, given that Matthew had been less than attentive all evening, she felt sure there wouldn't be any hint of romance in the car journey. He had not been rude, but he had chatted with everyone and not given any indication of interest in her. Part of her was a little disappointed that her dress had seemed to grab his attention early in the evening but then obviously had left him cold as he'd spent time with everyone else rather than her.

Still, she was so mixed up about her feelings she was grateful that Matthew's distance made it clear how he felt about her. This way working at the hospital would not get awkward. At best they were professional co-workers who enjoyed each other's company, and at worst he made it clear he didn't approve of the exchange and she would probably be the last overseas resident ever to work at the Eastern Memorial. It was just a little crush, she decided. A harmless crush that would quickly pass.

The object of her attention turned and caught her watching him. He had been deliberately avoiding Beth all evening. Just being near her was difficult for him as he wanted so much to reach out and pull her dangerously close. He fought his desire to take her home and slip that satin dress from her body and watch it fall to the floor as he pulled her into his arms and felt her soft skin next to his. But his head ruled his heart and that would not and could not happen. He could never let a woman come that close again. No, he would keep things friendly and professional even though tonight Beth was the most desirable woman he had ever laid eyes on.

'So, young lady, shall I get you home now?' Matthew said as he held his emotions in check and crossed the balcony to Beth.

Beth nodded and smiled to mask her disappointment. His tone was bordering on condescending, not unlike that of a big brother. He cut such a handsome figure and was undoubtedly the most charismatic man at the dinner party. She couldn't help but notice other women admiring him from a distance. She'd felt a strange sense of ownership more than once during the evening, and had mentally berated herself for thinking she had any reason to feel jealous. Matthew was nothing more than her boss and she was nothing more to him than a resident. And, as he had told her once, a disruption to the running of the hospital, she reminded herself.

'Let's be off, then,' he casually said as he took her arm and led her to the door.

They made their way to his car. The evening was still wonderfully warm and Beth was enjoying the fact that she had escaped a cold English winter.

He opened the car door for Beth then made his way to his side before he put the top down and made the car into a convertible for the trip home. 'I hope you don't mind but I thought it wouldn't matter if your hair gets a little messy on the way home. You arrived in pristine condition, thanks to the cab, but now that dinner is over we don't have to worry.'

'Not at all. It's far too nice an evening to drive with air conditioning on and the windows up.'

He took the car slowly out of the street then sped up when he reached the main road. Beth stared straight ahead. She didn't want to make eye contact. Should she read more into that comment? she wondered. Was he hinting at something? No, she decided he was being both polite and a gentleman and it was her imagination running amok. She decided to remain friendly but a little aloof. It was best all round.

'Seriously, Beth, a change in footwear couldn't be the driving force behind your move to Australia. Why here? And going back a little further, why medicine in the first place?'

Beth felt oddly secure with Matthew. The questions didn't appear intrusive but seemed to reflect a genuine interest.

'You probably heard me talking to Professor Rowe about my father. They studied together eons ago. My father's a vascular surgeon,' she replied without hesitation. 'I suppose I just followed him into medicine. I listened to his stories as a child and he seemed so passionate about what he did that I grew up thinking that being a doctor was the best job in the whole world.'

'And now?'

Beth smiled. 'And now I know it is.'

Matthew could see she meant every word. She loved practising medicine and it showed. 'And your family approved of you travelling to the other side of the world and working with a bunch of Aussies?'

Beth started shifting in her seat a little. It had been a lovely evening and she didn't want to go there and answered abruptly, 'I'm a big girl and I didn't really seek their approval.'

Matthew couldn't help but notice the change in her demeanour. She suddenly seemed agitated. He didn't want to probe but he thought there was something she wasn't saying. Discussing her family made her uncomfortable and he wondered why. But he left it alone. He respected her need to keep some things to herself. He certainly did.

They could both keep their secrets. That worked for him.

Matthew pulled up outside Beth's house and went around to open her door for her. Beth alighted from the car after taking Matthew's outstretched hand. As she stepped forward she suddenly caught her heel in a crack on the pavement. She felt herself toppling over and tried in vain to right herself. Matthew reached for her, catching her in his arms in mid-fall. She was so embarrassed she wanted to be swallowed up by the paving stones that tripped her.

Then she looked up into the eyes of her knight in shining armour and found that he didn't have a brotherly look any more. His eyes were intense and roaming her face. He gently brushed a stray wisp of hair from her forehead and then without warning kissed her. It was a kiss so tender that she lost her breath. He pulled her even closer and she felt powerless to move.

Suddenly she felt his warm hand in the

small of her back, his fingers touching her bare skin where the fabric of the bodice ended. Her heart raced and the intensity of her body's response surprised her. She had never felt his hands on her body, and nothing could have prepared her for the overwhelming desire that seized her. She felt light-headed but it was a wonderful feeling, as if his touch set electricity running through her body.

She kissed him with equal passion. Her reservations were lost the moment she felt his chest pressed hard against her. His strong arms wrapped around her made her feel tiny compared to his commanding body. He lifted his arm from the small of her naked back to her neck and his fingers freed her hair from the confines of the clasp. She felt the curls fall to her bare shoulders as she enjoyed his mouth savouring hers. She was vulnerable to this man as she had never been before. She didn't want it to stop.

Suddenly a car rounded the corner and the headlights shone on them. Matthew let his hands drop and he moved away as if he had been caught, and brought to his senses. As quickly as he had begun to seduce Beth, he ended it. He stepped back, wiping her lipstick from his mouth with the back of his hand as if it were toxic.

'I'm sorry,' he began. 'I don't know what came over me. That should never have happened.'

Beth stood in stunned silence.

'Are you all right?' he asked nervously, as he looked down at the pavement and her feet. 'You tripped and I tried to catch you.'

'I know...thank you. There must have been a crack in the footpath. I'm fine, truly I am.'

Matthew clenched his jaw tightly. He was angry with himself for what he had just done. He had allowed himself to be swept away by his feelings and he couldn't let that happen. 'I don't know what to say except that I overstepped the mark and it won't happen again. I apologise and I hope you can forgive me.'

'Really,' Beth cut in, 'there's no need to apologise, there's nothing to forgive.'

Beth was more disturbed than ever. Only a moment before she was being kissed in the most passionate way by a very handsome man and she'd enjoyed it. Now he stood before her apologising. Was it her? Had he suddenly found her undesirable?

'I must be going,' he said as he ran around to the driver's door. 'Are you all right to get inside?'

Beth fumbled for her keys in her evening clutch. She was shaking, not from the fall but from the kiss. She held up the keys and Matthew waited for her to get safely into her house, closing the door behind her, before he drove off into the night.

He didn't trust himself to be anywhere near her. He knew if he had stepped inside her house he might not have stopped what he had started. In fact, he knew he would not have stopped and that would spell disaster for him. He needed to keep a woman like Beth as far away as possible. Nothing good could come of it.

He couldn't risk falling in love. He had sworn five long years ago that being in love brought more heartache than joy. There was only one person in the world on whom he could depend and that was himself. He had learnt that the hard way. The moment he felt himself tempted to be close to Beth, to let her be an important part of his life, or any part of his life other than work, he had to remind himself of all he had to lose.

He couldn't ever depend on a woman. Because women ran away when the tough stuff of life reared its ugly head. The idea of couples staying together for better or for worse was a myth. If you fell on hard times you were left to do it alone. For that reason he had decided it was better just to be alone. Never to become involved. That way he couldn't be hurt or disappointed ever again.

Beth rested back against the closed front door as she dropped her clutch on the hallstand. She kicked her shoes off. The house was gently lit by the lamp in her bedroom. She looked in the entrance hall mirror and saw her hair was loose around her shoulders and her lipstick was smudged around her still quivering mouth. *What just happened?* She wasn't sure.

CHAPTER FIVE

'DR SEYMOUR, WE have a head trauma in exam bay three.'

Beth took the notes Yvette handed her and briefly read over them as she headed in the direction of the patient. The night before had been long and tortured, and sleep had not come easily. She'd relived the kiss over and over and then the tortured look on Matthew's face had come back to haunt her. It had almost been disgust she'd seen as he'd wiped his mouth with his hand. She had no idea what to make of it. He could have just steadied her and then stepped back. She hadn't thrown herself at him or forced him to kiss her.

Fortunately the reality of the afternoon shift in the emergency department gave her little time to think about the bizarre ending to her evening with Matthew.

'The medics just brought her in. Her name

is Kylie…she's late twenties, knocked over by a cyclist as she crossed the road. They applied a pressure bandage. She was unconscious at the scene but regained consciousness en route. They gave IV pethidine for pain. Her vitals are stable, BP one-ten over sixty, and she appears lucid.'

'Let's just ensure it's not a lucid interval,' Beth replied, noting the patient's hair was heavily matted with blood around the injury site. Beth slipped on her surgical gloves and approached the barouche. 'Kylie, my name is Dr Seymour. I need to ask you some questions.'

The young woman blinked and nodded but appeared in a slightly confused state.

'Please tell me your full name and date of birth,' Beth said as she took her pulse.

'Kylie Smith. Seventh of June….' She paused. 'Oh, hold on… Yes, yes, nineteen-eighty-five.'

'Do you remember what happened?' Beth asked as she attempted to remove part of the bandage to check the wound.

'Not really,' Kylie replied. 'I was shopping on King William Road with girlfriends and then I woke up in the ambulance. I feel fine. Can I go home now?'

'Not yet, Kylie,' Beth responded. 'Any

head injury that causes you to lose consciousness needs to be assessed and we will probably need to keep you in overnight.'

'But I'm fine. Seriously, let me go home. I don't have to stay…you can't force me to be here.'

'No, I can't make you. But I can advise you. At least let me look and give you my opinion. I may have to cut away some of the matted hair.'

Kylie raised her free hand to her head. 'Don't cut anything! I've got to be a bridesmaid next weekend and I'm not losing my hair.'

'I will try to work around it, but I can't guarantee you won't lose some hair.' Beth began to remove the bandage and found the skull to be slightly depressed. 'I'm afraid we are going to need X-rays and then we will transfer you to a ward for observation. With an injury of this nature I don't feel comfortable letting you return home today.'

The young woman moved as if to leave. 'I've got a hen's night tonight and I am not missing that to stay in here. I'm the party planner and she's my best friend. I need to be there. What's the worst that could happen… a rotten headache? I'll take some painkillers and be done with it.'

Beth was past being subtle with her prognosis. 'There's a chance that your brain may have been damaged by the blow to your head when you fell. We can't tell yet the extent of the injury. There's also the additional chance that you could suffer a haemorrhage inside the skull due to damage to the main artery, and you may lapse into a coma. If I were you, I wouldn't be going anywhere tonight, Kylie.'

On hearing the prognosis, the young woman immediately stopped arguing and lay back down with tears trickling down her cheeks. Beth didn't like being so harsh but if it saved a life she wouldn't hesitate.

She removed her latex gloves, completed her initial assessment notes and wrote an X-ray request. 'Yvette, can we get Kylie in for an immediate CAT scan? Depending on the results we may send her straight to ICU. Ask them to call me with the results stat. There's always a risk, however slight, of extradural bleeding from the middle mengineal artery or one of its branches. I won't take any chances on this.'

Yvette signalled the orderly to take Kylie to the X-ray department, leaving Beth with her thoughts. *A hens' night?* Seriously, the young woman had had a blow to the head, lost consciousness, risked a brain haemorrhage, and she was worried about missing out on some shots at a bar? Oh, and probably the prerequisite stripper… With that thought a sudden and most unwanted visual appeared in Beth's mind. It was a very chiselled stripper, his defined tanned abs oiled, his lean, taut body moving suggestively to music… Slowly the stripper was approaching her, nervously she lifted her eyes from his perfect body to find…Matthew's handsome face smiling back at her.

Beth gave herself a mental shake and headed back to the reception area. That was an image she didn't need on such a busy morning. What on earth had possessed her? It had been a kiss, nothing more, and now she was picturing him almost naked and it was only one o'clock in the afternoon. She needed to focus and get Matthew Harrison out of her head.

'Good afternoon, Dr Seymour.'

Beth raised her eyes to see Dan standing at the reception desk, smiling at her.

'So, how did the hot date go?'

Beth ignored his comment and reached for the next patient's notes.

'I know we haven't known each other very long, it's only day four, in fact, but if there's something you'd like to confide in me, I'm all ears.'

'Dan, knock it off,' came Yvette's voice across the desk as she held out some case notes. 'We've got a full house today so you can leave Beth alone and move on to the patients.'

'Nurses just don't show us any respect any more,' Dan said light-heartedly as he took the notes from Yvette. 'Anyway, as I was saying, Beth, I can be a sounding board for your spicy little affair. I personally have no love life, haven't for years. My high-school formal was my last hot date, so I can live vicariously through you!'

'I can't believe this place,' Beth began. 'Does anything personal ever remain that way?'

'Not if I can help it.' He shrugged and turned to the sea of waiting faces. 'Mrs Smithers?'

An elderly lady holding a handkerchief to her left eye approached Dan. He took her arm and escorted her to one of the examination bays. He popped his head back around the curtain to Beth.

'I have a rostered day off tomorrow, so don't you and Harrison get too cosy and set a wedding date while I'm away. The speed you're moving at, nothing would surprise me!'

Beth threw her hands up in disgust. As if she didn't have enough problems, without Dan's unsettling comments. He was like the brother she'd never had—irritating and obnoxious. But despite him teasing her at every opportunity, she did feel like she was part of a large, slightly intrusive but loving work family. A feeling of belonging somewhere. And that was a good feeling.

But Beth could already feel a knot of apprehension tightening in her stomach with the thought of seeing Matthew again.

'I must say,' Yvette began in a low voice, out of Dan's range, 'Dr Harrison is an utter nightmare at the best of times but awfully hot, almost as hot as the new ENT consultant. Now, I would totally enjoy seeing him lose his swim briefs in the surf!'

Beth was taken aback by Yvette's sudden confession, but she smiled with the image and felt so much better that she wasn't the only one imagining a co-worker *sans* clothing.

Suddenly two police came through the doors to the emergency department with a bedraggled and bloodied man in their custody. He was staggering and clearly under the influence of alcohol or some other substance.

'Need some help with this one,' the taller officer announced. 'Picked him up on North Terrace after a scuffle outside a bar. Think he might need stitches on his forehead and his mouth isn't looking too good. His BAC is just over point one seven.'

Beth directed them to the first available room and, donning her gloves, began an examination. Due to his intoxicated state the officers both remained while she administered a local anaesthetic then cleaned and sutured the wound to his head. His mouth was another matter, as he had lost both front teeth in the altercation. There was nothing Beth could do except clean the area, apply some gauze to control the bleeding and refer him to the dental hospital.

The officers escorted him out and down to the emergency department of the dental hospital not far away. She was unsure if there would be any disorderly conduct charges or if he would just spend the night in custody to allow the effects of the alcohol to wear off.

'Can you come to my office for a moment?'

Beth turned to see Matthew standing in the hallway leading to his office.

'Sure,' she muttered. She was not ready for this. She swallowed nervously as she followed him.

'Yvette, we'll just be a minute,' Matthew remarked as they headed down the corridor. Matthew closed the door behind them and crossed to his desk, where he leant with his arms folded across his chest. He needed to straighten out what had happened and make sure there was no misinterpretation. Not that a kiss could be seen in any light other than a kiss. A man attracted to a woman and acting on it. But he had to make sure Beth knew it would never happen again. He had slipped. He needed to resurrect the boundaries of the relationship and let Beth know how he felt.

'Beth, what happened last night was wrong, and I'm sorry. You said at the time you forgave me, and I hope that still holds,' he began as he rubbed the cleft of his chin with his hand. 'I admire you as a resident. Don't think for a minute I haven't noticed your work ethic and the way the patients respond to you, and I feel confident you can be an asset to the Eastern. You have changed my opinion about the exchange programme in a few short days and I think we have the basis of a good working relationship. How about we put last night behind us and start again?'

'Starting again sounds perfectly fine to me,' she said, not really knowing how else to respond. Turning to leave, she added, 'If that's all, I'll get back to the patients. There's still a few waiting.'

Matthew saw her turn away. He suddenly realised that everything he'd said was a lie. A lie he didn't want to stand by. He wanted to spend more time with her. He was at war with himself. He knew the possible casualties would be his heart and his sanity if he lost, but reason disappeared when she was around. The entire speech he'd delivered was about to be undone.

It was crazy but just being near Beth made him want to know more about her. She was different from any woman he had ever known. She was so passionate about medicine and her career. She stood up to him and didn't let him get away with being an insensitive tyrant. And he knew that was exactly what he had been for too many years. She was getting under his skin because she wasn't trying to. It was insane after such a short time to be thinking this way but he couldn't help himself. It was against his better judgement but he wanted to undo everything he'd just said and see Beth outside work. Everything he had rationally told himself during another sleepless night was about to ignored.

'What about dinner on Sunday?'

Beth stopped in her tracks. She wanted to say, *Are you quite mad?* But instead she answered, 'I don't think that's a very good idea. We should keep this to a working relationship and forget anything else.'

'I'm talking about going out just as friends. You're new to Adelaide and I can show you around. No strings and, I promise, no repeat of last night.' Then added confidently, 'I can pick you up at seven and have you home by nine.' This was just a man and a woman sharing a friendly dinner, he told himself.

Beth was completely baffled by this invitation, but for some crazy reason was unable to resist spending more time with Matthew, if only as friends. This certainly would be a test. She wasn't sure if she would be the only one tested after last night but for some inexplicable reason she couldn't say no.

'Seven it is,' she answered. 'I can make you a cup of English tea at my place afterwards. Are you thinking casual or are we donning our finest again?'

'Casual, the best wood-oven pizzas in town.'

Beth spent the next three days wondering what to make of the impending dinner. Friends? Was that even possible?

Matthew appeared happier in general. The staff noticed a difference in his demeanour. Dan, in particular, commented on returning from his day off that the A and E consultant was less like a dictator with each passing minute. He also couldn't resist teasing Beth about her part in Matthew's mood swing and his undying gratitude to her.

'Taking one for the team…' he said laughingly more than once.

No one knew if Matthew and Beth were seeing each other but they knew, whatever the relationship, it was making a difference at work. Beth denied anything but Dan said it was like he had landed back in a different hospital. He called her a miracle worker and in jest offered to kiss her feet.

Sunday came around quickly and Matthew arrived on time. He had questioned his own motives for the dinner. Friends? Even he didn't believe that story and he was the author. He enjoyed Beth's company and he wanted to see if he could spend time with her and not lose his heart. He couldn't afford to be hurt again, the very thought of being that vulnerable scared him to the core. However, he found himself thinking about her throughout the day and the night. He found reasons to bump into her at work and talk over cases. The work that had been his mistress for many years was no longer his only priority.

The evening was warm again but not humid. It was a dry heat, and Beth loved the weather, knowing she had left winter behind in London. Beth also enjoyed knowing that her stepfamily was on the other side of the world and unable to touch her new life.

She was finally stepping out of their shadow and experiencing a new life that she was loving more every day.

Beth had been excited about the date and seeing Matthew in an intimate social situation. Their last time together away from work had been the dinner at the Lancasters'. It had been anything but intimate. Tonight would be her chance to really get to know Matthew and she was very much looking forward to it.

She chose a simple floral strappy dress and flat gold sandals. Her hair was down in spiral curls around her shoulders—the humidity had won the war and straightening wasn't an option. She had a bright red clutch purse that matched the red hyacinth pattern on the dress. She couldn't wipe the smile from her face as she readied herself for her evening with Matthew. He was a handsome, charming man offering friendship—and perhaps, in time, more. But just spending time with Matthew was enough at the moment. He made Beth feel special as a woman and that was just what she needed.

'Beth, you look gorgeous,' Matthew told her as they took their seats at the restaurant. 'There won't be a man in the room tonight who won't wish he was me.' He was trying to remain friendly but detached but it wasn't working. She brought about a level of honesty he hadn't experienced in years.

'You're very sweet, Matthew, but I don't think so,' she said, as she tried to shield her eyes from his by nonchalantly surveying the room.

Matthew watched Beth looking everywhere but at him. He found her self-consciousness endearing. There were definitely many layers to this woman. She was intelligent, dedicated and when necessary feisty, but still not so sure of herself to take a compliment easily. He wondered why.

'So, pizza with the lot?' he asked.

'Anchovies?'

'Definitely, and olives?'

'Yes, please.'

They both smiled.

They nibbled on the warm garlic bread and Matthew ordered them each a glass of red wine.

'And your family were happy about your decision to travel?' Matthew asked as they waited for the pizza.

Beth smiled then sighed. 'I think my father was happy about the move.' She answered with a shrug. 'My mother passed away when I was ten and a year later my father remarried. Since then he has been pretty busy with work and his wife and stepdaughter. Hattie and Charlotte are a handful so I just get on with it.'

'I'm so sorry to hear about your mother.'

'It was a long time ago,' she said softly. 'But I still miss her terribly.'

'I'm sure you always will.'

Beth was touched by his response but didn't want dinner to turn into a pity party. She also wasn't ready to bare her soul, so she skimmed over the details. 'I'm fine really, I grew up quickly and learnt to make decisions for myself at a young age. My father hasn't always been available to me but he has certainly kept a lovely roof over my head and covered my education generously, so I'm grateful.'

'That sounds a bit lonely,' he said, looking into her eyes and sensing sadness. He was very close to his parents and he couldn't imagine it any other way. They had been his anchor through the tough times, his moral compass on quite a few occasions, and his sounding board since his childhood. 'I thought he'd be thrilled about you becoming a doctor and following in his footsteps. I'm surprised he wasn't involved with a huge decision like you leaving England.'

'I'm a big girl,' she retorted, looking away and reaching for her glass of wine. 'I'm twenty-eight, I do just fine without parental supervision.' She took a giant sip of the wine and feigned a smile.

Matthew could tell that Beth was feeling uncomfortable and a little defensive about the direction of their conversation so he shifted the focus to his family. He told her how his parents lived on the east coast of Australia. He talked about his trips to see them and how the two certified practising accountants had turned into new-age hippies in their retirement.

The mood lightened when he discussed their home in the rainforest, their new-found love of cheesecloth clothing and matching long grey hair. He chose not to discuss his ex-fiancée or anything about that time in his life. He was enjoying the evening too much to share any bad memories. Matthew was so happy to see Beth smiling and decided not to bring up her family again. There was much he wanted to ask but in turn she might ask about areas of his life he didn't want to recall, let alone discuss. No, he decided it would be best to let Beth open up about her family if she wanted to during the evening.

Beth was enjoying the date. She knew she had Matthew's undivided attention and even though it was more friendly than romantic it was a lovely evening. Beth noticed that Matthew never mentioned in passing any relationships. Not that she was expecting a tally or rundown of the women he had bedded, but she found it unusual that he never mentioned his personal life It was as though he deliberately chose to avoid the topic. Beth remembered Dan talking about an accident and a broken engagement, but Matthew made no mention of either.

'So, no boyfriend waiting back home for your return?' Matthew asked casually as he sipped his wine.

Beth almost choked on her garlic bread. The question came from nowhere but she liked the idea that he cared to know if there was one.

'No, none worth talking about.' Beth didn't know why she had put it that way. Perhaps it was her surprise at being asked that had thrown her. 'No, actually, none at all.' She laughed.

'Now, that I find hard to believe.' Matthew was relieved that there was no one in her life but he didn't know what he wanted to do about it. He would have been jealous if she had told him there was a man waiting for her return, but at the same time he didn't want to act on the fact Beth was single. He wished he could get past the need to protect himself from falling in love.

'Dr Harrison, Dr Matthew Harrison.'

Beth felt her heart tug a little as he moved away to face the direction of the monotone voice.

'There's an urgent telephone call for you in the lobby.'

Beth turned to see the waiter standing at the door and Matthew rising from his chair.

'I turned off my mobile phone but left the restaurant name with the paging service in case of an emergency,' he said as he rose from the table. 'Excuse me, please, I shouldn't be long.' He left the table, pausing briefly to smile back in Beth's direction. The serious Dr Harrison took over as he rushed from the room, questioning the immaculately attired messenger.

The spell was broken. But she hoped it was only for a moment.

Beth stared into space. Her fellow restaurant patrons were immersed in conversations around her, but Beth was happy to be alone in the crowded room with her thoughts. Warm, delicious thoughts of Matthew.

The aroma of the wood-oven pizza preceded the waiter and was overwhelming as it was placed before Beth with extra, freshly grated parmesan cheese. Five minutes passed, with the delectable food sitting untouched in front of her. There was still no sign of Matthew so Beth removed her napkin from her lap and went to find him.

She came upon him pacing the hallway, the cordless telephone at his ear.

'There's no one, you're sure?'

She knew better than to interrupt, and a nervous smile curved her lips as she caught his attention. His eyes roamed appreciatively over her but his smile in return was half-hearted and distracted.

'Well, then, it seems that there's no choice. I'll be there in ten minutes. Let's hope for their sake it's soon enough.' With that he put the telephone back in its cradle and stared for a moment at Beth in silence. His mind, she guessed, was elsewhere.

'Is there anything I can do?'

'No. It's just routine hospital mayhem,' he said, rubbing his lined brow. 'I step away for five minutes and the place falls to pieces. Seems like Berketta and Sanderson have been sick-listed with gastro problems since five-thirty and there's an RTA heading in. I'll have to go and give the others a hand.'

'I can come too,' said Beth, trying to keep up with his long strides as he made his way to the front door.

'No need,' he said matter-of-factly, and headed to the restaurant door. 'You have worked more than enough hours this week. Just stay here and enjoy dinner. I shouldn't be too long and I don't want you to miss out on the best pizza in town after the hype I gave it.'

Beth looked away in disappointment. She knew it was part of Matthew's job. Being a doctor meant being called away and a social life coming second. She accepted she had no right to complain but she turned to walk away before her emotions betrayed her.

'There is one thing before I go,' he said, suddenly sweeping her into his arms. 'This.'

Bending low, he kissed her so tenderly she felt her breath was stolen. Her eyes closed as his hands moved slowly, repeatedly, over the curves of her bare shoulders and she felt the beating of his heart through the thin material of his shirt. She was drowning in the sweetness of his mouth as he took her and she was powerless to control her response. She wanted him closer, yet he was already crushing her thin dress against his hard chest. His lips moved forcefully, yet still tenderly, parting hers as the kiss deepened, and she sensed a need in him that only Beth Seymour the woman, not the capable medical resident, could satisfy. She wanted to be with this man more than anything she had wanted in her life.

Abruptly he released her from his embrace. Beth swayed for a moment as she tried to steady her trembling legs and calm her racing heart.

'I've been dying to do that since I first saw you tonight,' he said raggedly. 'I don't know where this is going, or if it will go anywhere, but I had to do it.' Matthew had finally let his heart drive his actions. He had surprised himself but it felt good. 'And I am not about to apologise again.'

Beth pursed her bruised lips in stunned silence.

'Please keep my seat warm and enjoy the pizza. Yvette said no one's listed as critical.'

'Let me help,' she managed to say.

'You can do as you're asked, Dr Seymour,' he said, gently placing his finger on her lips to silence her. 'Don't worry, I'll be back, you can count on it. You promised me a proper cup of tea at your place.'

He took the keys to his car from the concierge, leaving Beth alone and feeling dazed.

From the corner of her eye she noticed the waiter staring in the most curious way and she realised why. The kiss. Her lipstick. What must she look like? With her hand patting the corners of her mouth self-consciously, she asked her host directions to the powder room to correct her make-up. He gladly obliged, but to Beth's consternation his puzzlement had turned into a knowing smile.

Her mind was constantly on Matthew for the next hour. She finished two slices of the pizza and the waiter brought her a complimentary lemon gelato. Beth looked wistfully at Matthew's glass sitting untouched on the table. She hoped any moment he would reappear, sweep her into his car and drive into the night. She prayed the magic between them wouldn't be dampened by the clinical reality of A and E.

She followed the paved path that led from the indoor section of the restaurant to an ivy-covered gazebo. Small garden lights dotted the way and a number of guests were sitting on benches scattered along the pathway. She felt glad to be alone with her thoughts.

Her rose-coloured glasses slipped for a moment as she wondered if she was being too hopeful. She sat down in the gazebo and looked up through the vines to the crescent moon in the clear night sky. Her reasoning self fought with her heart until the memory of the fire and passion in his kiss told her to drive away her doubts once and for all. There had been nothing platonic about Matthew's actions tonight.

Finally the concierge approached Beth with a message. Matthew wasn't coming back but he had arranged a cab to get her home. She came back to reality with a thud. This was not how it was supposed to turn out. Not even close. Beth couldn't believe that she was just getting close to this man and he was taken from her by duty. She couldn't have been more disappointed. She could still feel his kiss on her lips and his arms around her as he had swept her off her feet. She was devastated that the evening had ended this way. Where might the evening have led without the interruption? she wondered as she picked up her bag and slowly made her way through the busy restaurant to the waiting cab. But this night she would be spending alone.

Beth woke in the morning and checked her mobile to see if there was a message from Matthew. There was nothing. She was disappointed that he hadn't sent a text to let her know whether he intended coming over for tea. She had waited up till nearly eleven before heading to bed. With a lot on her mind, particularly the kiss before Matthew had left the restaurant, Beth had thought she would toss all night, but the moment her head had hit the pillow, she'd fallen asleep.

She had been so tired after six straight days at the hospital that she'd slept like a log and hadn't woken up till late. But her first waking thoughts were of Matthew. She wanted to pick up the phone and call him, but she resisted. She had done enough of trying to get attention for one lifetime. Matthew needed to be the one who reached out. He had still left her sitting alone in the restaurant, so he needed to make the first move. Her chasing days were over.

Matthew returned to her home just before eleven o'clock. Beth's lights were still on. He turned off the engine and looked at the house. Suddenly the reality hit him. Who was he kidding? He didn't want a cup of tea. He wanted Beth. She was a desirable woman and he would not be able to stop himself. He had already felt the softness of her skin and tasted the sweetness in her kiss. If she didn't stop him he would make love to her, over and over again. No longer would he be Beth's boss, or her friend. They would be lovers.

Matthew sank back in the car seat. He couldn't do it. He had raced back to be with her but now, as he thought it through, he knew he couldn't allow himself to get that close. This wasn't a one-night stand. Beth was definitely a relationship waiting to happen and he wasn't ready to take that on. He couldn't become involved. That might actually make him dependent on another human being.

Matthew wished he had not been called back to the hospital. If he had spent the evening with Beth, then maybe, just maybe he would not have had the time to think. He knew thinking was his worst enemy. He reached for the ignition, paused for a moment to look at Beth's house, then started the engine and drove slowly down the quiet street. He wished with what was left of his heart that things could be different.

CHAPTER SIX

WITH AN ENTIRE two days to herself, and determined to forget Matthew's failure to return to her, or even to call, Beth decided she needed a distraction. He was desperately close to claiming her heart, but she also knew she couldn't sit around waiting for him. She would most certainly go mad if she didn't think about something else.

A suitable diversion, she decided, was shopping for some new summer clothes. She had brought a few things with her but the Australian summer was far warmer than she was accustomed to, and she had a few more months before the cooler weather arrived.

She rang Yvette at the hospital to ask the best shopping destinations and was given a few options. It seemed Adelaide was quite the shopping Mecca according to her new friend. Yvette suggested Rundle Street would be the closest and Beth took her advice. Dressed in her only pair of shorts, a knitted cotton top and sandals, she caught a tram to town. Even though she wasn't a big shopper by nature, she soon found a few pieces that caught her eye, including a couple of sundresses, a new bag and two pairs of flat sandals. The shop assistants were very helpful and Beth enjoyed a few hours of retail therapy before she sat down at a restaurant for lunch al fresco.

She had checked her mobile a number of times and there had been nothing from Matthew. She was disappointed, but she refused to let it ruin her day. He had her number but for some reason he wasn't using it. Matthew was complicated, and that was something she couldn't change. He'd made it clear that he was crossing over the line of friendship before he ran off into the night without a word. But there wouldn't be a third kiss without an explanation and/or apology. If his lips met hers again it wouldn't be by accident or sudden infatuation. Beth needed to know that there was some meaning behind the next kiss. If he wasn't comfortable with his feelings then she was happy to let him go. She wanted to be the focus of a man's attention, not the reason for his distress.

Beth ordered a fresh tomato and basil bruschetta with a cappuccino while she sat outside in the shade of the grape vines, people-watching. She was intrigued to see the relaxed way the Australians dressed and went about their shopping. Although Adelaide was a city, it lacked the hurried bustle of London. It was as though everyone was on holiday.

'A penny for your thoughts?'

Beth's coffee cup dropped to the table as she turned to see Matthew standing beside her.

'How did you find me?' she responded, not trying to mask the irritation she was feeling.

'I overheard Yvette telling Dan where you were spending your day off. I needed to pick up some dry cleaning down the street so thought I'd make my way in here and see if I bumped into you.'

He hadn't wanted to call her and make plans. He'd wanted it to be more casual. An almost accidental meeting.

He didn't want to need her. He wasn't ready to commit to anything. He decided to keep it friendly. That way he could enjoy Beth's company but not risk his heart. A friend couldn't break his heart like a lover, he'd decided.

Despite herself, Beth was happy to see Matthew. She was still annoyed and puzzled by his lack of a text or phone call the previous night, but there was something about the man that made her want to be in his company. She noticed him smiling at her—almost laughing.

'Why are you looking at me like that? What's so funny?'

Without saying a word, Matthew leant over and wiped the frothy moustache from her top lip with his crisp white handkerchief. He tried not to touch her skin with his fingers. He knew it would be warm and soft, and he didn't want to be tempted again.

Beth instantly flinched, feeling quite silly.

'Madam had a little something on her lip,' he remarked with a casual smile.

'I could have done that myself, but thank you.'

'You're welcome,' Matthew knew Beth was annoyed, and admitted to himself that she had every reason to be.

'So what happened last night?' she asked flatly. 'I ate pizza alone, and I understand that the hospital must always come first, but then I boiled the kettle and drank my tea alone at home without a call or a text.' The tea bit wasn't exactly true but she had put out the teapot and cups before she'd given up waiting and gone to bed. She didn't want to appear so desperate that she would accept bad manners. Beth was not about to settle for scraps of attention from a man confused by his own feelings.

'I'm sorry that I kept you up,' Matthew started as he pulled out the chair and sat down opposite Beth, 'but I need to be honest. I'm not sure if it would have been the right thing for me to have come back last night.'

His expression was sombre. He knew he was probably making a huge mistake. Sitting opposite him was a beautiful woman and he was unable to give her what she deserved. He couldn't just give her one night because he actually cared about her. He knew he couldn't make love to her and then walk away. He realised just how much he felt for her.

Beth was confused. 'What do you mean?'

'Now's not the time to go into it,' he answered, as he abruptly stood, very aware of their less than private surroundings. 'You just have to believe when I say that it's best that I didn't come back to your place. Best for you and best for me.' He bent down and tenderly kissed her forehead then walked away, disappearing into the sea of people making their way through town.

Beth sat alone for what seemed the longest time. He'd kissed her on her forehead. Her forehead. Not her cheek and definitely not her lips. The forehead was the death knell for any romance. She knew that sort of kiss was relegated by men to extended family, like elderly, frail grandmothers or even babies. But lovers? Never.

Beth was devastated. She wished Matthew had never kissed her at all. Now he had kissed her three times. Twice it had been with passion. Twice she had felt her body come to life. Twice she had ached for more.

And once she had felt nothing. How could she feel anything from a kiss on the forehead?

Matthew walked swiftly back to the hospital. He didn't want to talk at an open-air restaurant. He didn't want to explain to Beth why he couldn't be more than her friend with an audience of strangers. He wasn't sure he wanted to explain at all.

As he entered A and E, he knew he owed her more, but he didn't want to get involved. She was sweet and gorgeous and he wanted to make love to her but he didn't want to fall in love with her. Walking away was the decent thing to do, he decided. But he needed to let her know it wasn't her. It was most definitely him.

Beth heard her phone ringing in her bag. She was still sitting at the table, trying to piece together the events of the last twenty-four hours.

'Hello.'

'Beth, it's Matthew.'

Beth stared into space, completely bemused as to why he would be calling. He had been with her less than ten minutes earlier and he'd left.

'I want to explain what just happened.'

'Then be my guest,' she retorted. 'I'm certainly listening.'

'Not on the phone. Can I come over tonight so we can talk? I think you deserve to know where I'm coming from.'

'Do you think there's any point in it? You're not interested in me. You made that clear.'

'It's not that black and white,' he said. 'There's more to it and I want you to know it's not you.'

'Ah, yes,' she answered, taking a deep breath. 'Time for the it's-not-you-it's-me speech.'

Matthew was desperate for Beth to know that it was the truth in this case. He had baggage enough for an entire bus and he wasn't about to explain all of it, but he could open up about it enough for her to realise she was not the problem. Far from it.

'Please give me an hour and I will explain what I can. I don't want to throw away what could be a great friendship.'

Beth realised she was still on an emotional roller-coaster with Matthew and she decided to take a final ride. 'Okay,' she agreed reluctantly as she absentmindedly played with her paper napkin. 'I should be home by six.'

'What if I pick up some fish and chips and see you around seven?'

'If that's what you want to do,' she answered him flatly. His behaviour had already undermined her fragile belief in herself as a woman. She just wanted a man to love and cherish her, to make her the centre of his world. Clearly Matthew was not going to be that man. The reason didn't really matter. He wasn't to be her Prince Charming.

As the night before, Matthew was right on time when he rang the doorbell. She opened the door and spied a bouquet of yellow roses in his arms and a large paper bag, presumably containing fish and chips, by his side.

'Hello, Beth. These are for you.' His smile was tentative as he placed the bouquet in her arms.

'Thank you. Please come inside,' she said as she stepped back from the door and lowered her head to smell the perfume of the flowers. Then she raised her eyes to meet his and added with a smirk, 'Are these from you, or the grateful parents of another patient?'

'These are most definitely from me. It's a peace offering for what I put you through last night. Having to cab it home alone definitely needs flowers to make it right.'

He thought back to that day a week ago when he had arrived at Beth's front door, using the flowers as an excuse to see her and then pretending there had been no room for the flowers at the hospital. But now he had to set things right. He had led her on but that had to stop. He hoped they could remain friends after tonight. He had hoped he could look past the hurt and give Beth more than friendship, but that wasn't to be.

'I hope you like roses.'

'My absolute favourite flower in the world,' she proclaimed honestly as she closed the door on the evening heat. Matthew was making an effort and she felt she needed to acknowledge that. Friendship was not what she wanted but it was better than no relationship at all, she surmised. And definitely an improvement on the first day at the hospital when he'd hollered at her. He had come a long way.

'My mother had a garden full and I just adored the perfume when I played outside as a child. We would often pick them and fill the house.'

'I'm glad,' he said, aware of how Beth still missed her mother. He intended to ask her more about her family during the evening, if she let him stay long enough. Friends should know such things about each other, he told himself.

'I need to find a vase,' Beth said softly. She hoped there was one in the furnished house. It had everything else so she assumed a vase would be in a cupboard somewhere. After rummaging in the kitchen, Beth emerged with the roses in a tall glass vase. Her mother had once told her that yellow roses signified the promise of a new beginning. She hoped that was what Matthew had meant when he'd chosen them.

'Thank you again, they're beautiful,' she said, and kissed Matthew lightly on the cheek as she passed by him on the way to place the roses on the table by the window. She was surprised by her own action. She hadn't thought it through, it had just seemed natural. It had just happened. She hoped it didn't send him scuttling away.

Matthew was taken aback for a moment.

He didn't want to read anything into the kiss.
He reminded himself that he had kissed her
on the forehead earlier on. It was the same.
Not romantic at all, just a sign of affection.

'Dinner…' he announced, holding up a bag
with two white boxes inside. 'I chose barramundi. Hope you like it.'

Beth smiled. Matthew was trying so hard.
She wasn't angry any more. Disappointment
still ran in her veins, but no animosity.

'I'm sure I will love it. Thank you.'

She crossed to the small dining table and
chairs. The table was set. Beth had put out
wine glasses, a bottle of fruity chardonnay
and some sourdough bread she had picked up
at the store. There was a tossed green salad
and a small glass bowl filled with olives.

They were two friends enjoying dinner.

'I'm not sure if it will be as good as your
English fish and chips,' he remarked as he
pulled the two boxes from the bag and placed
them on the table.

Beth carefully opened the first box and
lifted the hot fish from the box with some
serving tongs and placed one large fillet on
each plate before serving up the chips. Matthew took the bag and boxes into the kitchen
and returned to find Beth pouring some wine.

It felt comfortable. It felt nice. He felt safe.

They both sat down, placed their napkins on their laps and began eating. The fish was delicious and it melted in Beth's mouth. So fresh and only lightly battered. The chips were crisp and golden brown.

Matthew squeezed a lemon wedge over his food and from the corner of his eye he watched Beth enjoying the food. He decided to chat about work and not rush into his friendship spiel. That could wait. He was enjoying Beth's company.

'So, my newest resident, is A and E where you intend staying or do you want to specialise in another field?' he asked as he sipped the chilled wine.

Beth thought for a moment. 'To be honest, I had originally planned to follow my father into vascular surgery. But I find A and E a satisfying challenge so I'm fairly keen to keep on this path.'

Matthew was happy to know she enjoyed the work in A and E. He couldn't imagine being anywhere else. It was his passion and for the longest time it had been his life. His reason to get up in the morning when there was no other reason to. A and E never disappointed him. It never let him down and it gave him all he needed to feel alive.

'What about you? Had you ever planned

on specialising in another area?' she asked as she placed some salad on Matthew's plate, moved the olive bowl closer to him, then served herself some salad.

Matthew smiled at the way Beth had just naturally dished up his food. As though they had been sharing meals together for a long time. It felt relaxed. It felt right.

'No, A and E is definitely the place for me,' he replied.

There was so much Matthew got out of working in the emergency department, and so little it demanded. He could utilise his skills as a doctor without getting too close or attached to the patients. It was like a never-ending medical conveyer belt. It was challenging and fulfilling professionally to be able to save the lives of so many injured people and yet never know anything much about their personal lives. They were patched up and they left. Moved to surgery or a ward or sent home. No attachment. No fear of getting involved and no risk of getting hurt. For him it was the perfect place to work.

'Do you have any interests outside medicine?' he asked, before he took the last bite of the barramundi fillet. 'Like hunting pheasants or something else the English gentry do on their estates?'

'Pheasants, really.' Beth laughed. 'I love it that you're not tempted to stereotype.'

'Me? Never.' He smiled as put down his knife and fork, his eyes never leaving her face. It had been a long time since he'd felt this relaxed with anyone other than his immediate family.

'Actually, when I get time off, I love to watch old movies—'

'And shop a little,' he cut in as a smirk tugged the corners of his mouth.

Matthew watched the far-away look in Beth's eyes. She was beautiful, no doubt, but there was more that attracted him to spend time with her. He sensed she was trying to be strong and independent, and yet she was so warm and giving. She had her own walls up and he had no idea why.

'So apart from your Woodstock-loving parents and your musical sister, do you have any other family?' she asked as she gently placed her glass on the table and turned her attention back to her salad and remaining chips.

'No, that's it,' he announced. 'Although I often wish I had a larger family. It would be great to have those big family Christmas dinners with a dozen people at the table. But I don't have any complaints. We're close and there might be only four of us but we make enough racket when we get together for a dozen or more.'

Matthew thought momentarily of his ex-fiancée, and how the family had swelled to five for a while. But that had been short-lived and tonight he was not about to dwell on unpleasant memories. He was determined to move past that. He had to. He wanted to live in the present and the future and leave the past where it belonged. He would never be able to have that close, romantic relationship but he could still enjoy a woman's company. Tonight was proof of that.

Beth was happy to hear that Matthew was close to his family. That was extremely important to her. She had often wished she had full siblings, not just the type that fell into your lap, your closet and your diary when your father remarried. In her experience that was a worse scenario than being an only child. One day she wanted to have children of her own but vowed to have a brood of at least four. She wanted them to feel the love of a sibling the way she never had. She knew that some step-siblings enjoyed wonderful relationships but unfortunately she wasn't one of them.

'I forgot something,' Matthew said. 'Please

excuse me.' With that he stood and made his way to the front door. He fumbled with the keys in the lock, and finally opening the door he rushed out, closing it behind him.

Beth felt her stomach tighten and a sinking feeling engulf her. Was he leaving already? It didn't make sense. She hadn't put any pressure on him. They had been enjoying a pleasant evening. At least in her mind it had been enjoyable. But now she began to doubt herself. Was she dull? Had she read more into it? Was he just filling in time? Her insecurities were heightened in a matter of seconds.

Until she heard the front door open again.

Matthew rushed past her with a cold bag in his hands. 'I'll be just a minute,' he announced before disappearing into her tiny kitchen.

Beth heard rustling and then a cupboard being opened and closed, followed by the clunk of a plate on the stone bench. Next she heard drawers being opened and closed until finally she heard some cutlery being collected. She smiled. She had totally overreacted. He was preparing something but she had no idea what. He brought out two small plates and forks and put them on the table then collected the dinner dishes and salad bowl and walked back into the kitchen without saying a word.

His head appeared in the door opening. 'Just one more minute. Delicate operation in here.'

Beth sat with baited breath, hearing him humming to himself and searching the drawers again. 'Do you have—? Never mind, found it.'

Finally the humming and kitchen sounds ceased and Matthew appeared in the doorway.

'Pavlova!'

'Oh, my goodness!' Beth exclaimed as she spied the enormous cream and fruit covered dessert. 'I shall literally roll into work tomorrow after all I've eaten. Not that I am complaining, it's all delicious.'

'Hardly,' Matthew replied as he placed a mammoth slice of dessert on Beth's plate.

'That's too much, I can only imagine the calories!' she exclaimed, before raising her fork to sample the white fruity decadence.

'We can work it off later…'

Beth almost choked on the soft meringue as she thought of working off dinner later with Matthew. She knew he didn't mean it the way it had sounded, but she could dream. 'We can take a walk round the block. It's still

warm out,' he announced, as he took his first
bite of the creamy creation. He hadn't noticed
the colour change in Beth's cheeks.

'Wonderful,' she said, as she took another
bite of dessert, her wicked thoughts of working off the calories were dashed in seconds.

They decided against coffee, bursting with
the food they had eaten, so they packed the
dishes into the dishwasher and left for a walk
in the balmy evening air. The breeze was still
warm and it was a perfect night.

It was the most content Matthew had felt
in a long time, he felt like a weight had been
lifted from him. Like he was able to have fun
and enjoy Beth's company without being sus-
picious or feeling pressured.

He sat on the park bench and gently pulled
Beth down next to him. His look was playful but there was a serious undertone. 'Tell
me more about your stepfamily.'

'Now, why would you want to go and ruin
a perfectly lovely evening?' she said.

Matthew frowned. 'Because I want to
know more about you.'

Beth hesitated. 'Well, as I told you, my
father remarried when I was ten. My stepmother, Hattie, is nothing like my mother,

unfortunately. She's not the warmest person I've met—quite the opposite, in fact.'

Matthew could tell Beth was holding back. There was more to the story than just an unpleasant stepmother. There was something she wasn't saying.

'You don't get along?'

'I don't really factor in her life, so I can't say we don't get along. I rarely saw her. She was always flitting in and out with her charity lunches and meeting Charlotte's needs and I guess I was just there somewhere in the mix called my new family.'

'But your father was there for you, wasn't he?'

'He was dragged into all of Charlotte's dramas so he couldn't really be there for me too. He had to keep Hattie happy. He'd lost his wife and didn't want to lose Hattie too. It all got a bit much, so I decided to have a break from it and head Down Under for a while. I don't think I'll be missed, to be honest.'

Matthew was surprised by Beth's response. 'Kudos to your father for trying to let your stepsister know he cared about her troubles, but in the process you felt unimportant. That's wrong and he should know it. It's his duty to make you feel loved. I know he lost his wife, I understand that he felt alone and maybe wanted to have someone in his life again. But, Beth, you lost your mother that same day. You couldn't replace her.'

Beth was silent for a moment. Matthew was the first person to ever acknowledge the pain and loss she'd suffered. It was nice to finally have someone understand that her needs had been overlooked, but she felt she had to defend her father. It was still how she saw it after all these years. She believed they were both victims.

'I guess so, but he's a man trying to keep the peace and doing the best job he can.'

Matthew didn't see it that way at all.

'I beg to differ about that, but he's your father and it's not my place to say anything more.' Matthew didn't want to add to Beth's woes about her family. He respected that she wanted to keep her father on a pedestal and he wasn't about to launch an attack on the man who had raised her and inadvertently brought her to Australia. She was a long way from home and that wouldn't be fair.

He would keep his opinion about George to himself.

'I'm glad you came to Adelaide,' he said, 'whether it was to wear sandals or to get away from Hattie and Charlotte.'

He meant every word. But he needed to say something else.

'Beth, while we're baring our souls, we need to talk about last night.'

Beth bit her lip and prayed it wasn't about to become the nice-knowing-you speech. She had just opened up like never before and she felt quite vulnerable. Matthew was a wonderful man and as much as she was disappointed that he didn't want to pursue a romance, she would be even more upset if she couldn't be a part of his life as a friend.

Matthew stood and paced anxiously in front of her before he stopped and looked into her eyes. Something about her connected so deeply inside him. But he couldn't move on it. His thoughts were suddenly jumbled as he looked into the warmth of her brown eyes. *No*, he told himself. *You can't fall for her.*

Hearing about her family made him want to wrap his arms around her and protect her from the world, but he couldn't. He couldn't be drawn into anything even close to a romantic relationship. The kisses they had shared had been minor slips on his part. Despite the pain he knew she had suffered growing up, he had his own demons and all he could offer was friendship. But it was a genuine friendship. He could not make up for her father and stepmother making her feel second best, no one could, but he could be a shoulder to lean on if she needed him.

'It would have been wrong for me to come back to your place last night.'

'I'm not sure why you would say that.' Shaking her head, she questioned his statement. 'You came over tonight.'

He nodded. 'Yes, but tonight is different. Tonight we're spending time together as friends but last night would have had a very different ending if I'd had anything to do with it.'

Beth stared at him in silence. She wasn't sure where he was heading.

'I'm not ready for a relationship, Beth. I don't know if I ever will be. I don't want to lead you on. I'm pretty much destined to be a bachelor forever. Relationships and marriage will never be in the cards for me.'

'That sounds so bleak. To never see yourself in a relationship.' She looked at him with a frown. She thought about what he was saying and wondered if he was just being kind. Was he hiding behind his words? Did he not want to hurt her with the truth? She would rather rip the plaster off quickly than have it removed slowly. The result would be the same but it wouldn't be so drawn out. 'Is this because we work together or is it me?'

Matthew looked at the beautiful woman before him. How could she possibly think it was about her? No, he knew exactly why. Her family had made her feel second best. She was pretty, intelligent, funny and desirable yet apparently she was never seen or appreciated for the wonderful woman she was by those closest to her.

'No, Beth,' he said. Shaking his head and venturing close again, he sat down on the bench beside her. 'Believe me, I would be the luckiest man in the world to be dating you. I don't want to go into it, but I'm not relationship material. And you're not one-night-stand material, and therein lies our problem.'

Beth wasn't sure if this was the time but she decided to open up about what she knew and jump right in with both feet. She had been open and honest about her family and if Matthew was ending it before it began, she decided she had nothing to lose. 'Does this have anything to do with your broken engagement?'

His posture suddenly went rigid and defensive and the expression on his rugged face matched. Her comment sent shock waves through him. He had thought he could gently let Beth know that he wasn't available without too much detail about the reason. This was not in the plan.

'How do you know about that?' He ran his fingers nervously through his hair and looked down at the grass near his feet.

'It doesn't matter how I know,' she said. She noticed his darkening demeanour and, suddenly doubting her decision to bring it up, her voice wavered. 'If you don't want to talk about it, we can forget it. It's really not my business, or anyone else's for that matter.'

Matthew hadn't planned on discussing his ex-fiancée with Beth. He hadn't really planned on discussing her with anyone. He'd thought that part of his life could be buried, but apparently it was hospital gossip. 'It's complicated and messy and you probably don't want to know about it.'

'I want to hear whatever you want to tell me,' she said softly. 'Nothing more, nothing less.'

Matthew closed his eyes and thought that perhaps enough time had passed. Maybe he should talk about what had happened all those years ago. It wouldn't change anything, any more than Beth talking about her family could change what had happened to her. The past had shaped them both. Beth had risen above hers, left it behind her. He was still shackled to his.

He momentarily went back to that dark place that had almost engulfed him all those years ago.

'It's true I was engaged, about five years ago,' he began in earnest, staring into the distance but not seeing anything. 'Her name was Anne and she was Canadian. It all happened quickly but ended even faster. Let's just say she chose not to stick around when the going got tough.'

Matthew suddenly found it unnerving to talk about his fiancée, and wanted to keep his explanation brief. Baring his soul wouldn't change anything. He really liked Beth but it wouldn't be fair to let her think there was a chance for anything more than friendship. That was the only choice Anne had left him.

'But one broken engagement shouldn't stop you being in another relationship.'

'You wouldn't think so,' he conceded, 'but I don't want to make another woman pay for what that woman did.'

Beth's frustration was building. Not only was he being evasive, he was throwing away the chance for happiness because a woman had left him. It seemed ridiculous to her.

'So she broke your heart and now you want to spend the rest of your life alone?'

'I don't want to be alone,' he retorted. 'It's just the way it is.'

CHAPTER SEVEN

'LET'S WALK SOME more,' Matthew said, standing up and reaching for Beth's hand.

Beth knew better than to read anything more into it than just polite encouragement to leave the bench where they had been sitting. She accepted his hand and revelled in the warmth as their skin touched. The strength of his grip and the heat in his touch made her body tingle. She knew he didn't feel the same. She wanted so much to feel the strength and heat from his entire body as he took her and made love to her all night. But she knew that would never happen.

He released his hold when she was on her feet and began walking towards the main road.

'I hope you understand where I'm coming from now,' he said, while looking ahead. 'No need to dwell on what might have been.

I think you are an extraordinary woman and I hope we can really be friends.'

Matthew wished that weren't the case. He wanted to be so much more, he wanted to be able to reach out to Beth. To hold her tightly while they walked together in the moonlight. But he couldn't. He didn't have the emotional capacity to love. More to the point, he didn't have the reserves to survive if it didn't work out.

'Friends it is,' she answered softly, looking in the same direction. Straight ahead. She wanted to reach out, to put her hand in his hand and walk under the stars with the man she thought she was falling in love with, but she knew she couldn't. He wasn't available. He had built walls around his heart. At that moment she hated Anne, even though she didn't know her. She hated what the woman had done to inflict pain so deeply that Matthew didn't believe he would be able to give or receive love again.

They walked in silence for a few minutes, each deep in thought, each wanting the person next to them so badly but both unable to reach out.

Beth saw Matthew rub his temple more than once during the walk.

'Migraine?'

'No,' he replied. 'Just a common or garden variety headache. Probably too much sugar in the pavlova.' His mouth curved slightly but Beth could see his smile was subdued by the pain.

Matthew knew that sugar had nothing to do with it. Emotions and tension were the cause. He was anxious and battling himself, and his neurons had followed suit and begun waging war on each other. He needed to get some pain relief.

'Is there a chemist around, or should I head back to the car?'

Beth pointed ahead. 'There's one on the next corner. It's a twenty-four-hour pharmacy. They'd have codeine.'

Matthew nodded and they walked to the edge of the park and crossed the main road.

'I won't be selfish, Beth,' he said, as he looked into her eyes. 'I don't want to take up any more of your evening. I'll get the codeine and walk you home. Then I'll be out of your hair. There's only so much a resident can take of the boss, I'm sure.'

Beth's face clouded. She could take so much more of her boss, but he wasn't offering it.

She pressed the lights to the pedestrian

crossing and they waited in silence again. There was so much she wanted to say but she knew Matthew didn't want to hear any of it. He had made up his mind and she was reluctant to raise the matter again. Being friends was the only option on offer.

Matthew massaged his temples again. She knew the headache wasn't about to subside any time soon. They crossed on the green light and entered the pharmacy. Very swiftly, Matthew found what he was looking for and approached the counter to be served. As his purchase was rung up he saw the pharmacist on his knees in front of an elderly patient who was sitting on a chair near the dispensary.

'Mrs Downer, you will need to go to the hospital. There is nothing I can do for you. I think you need to be seen as soon as possible.'

'But I just need something for my indigestion,' the elderly woman said breathlessly. 'Then I can go home and get some sleep. I have to be up early to take care of Stanley. I'm babysitting him.'

'Mrs Downer, you had a pacemaker inserted only two days ago, so I don't think you should be ignoring any pains in your chest. I think it is more serious than just indigestion.'

Matthew took his change and put his purchase in his pocket and he approached the pair with Beth close by. 'Excuse me,' Matthew interrupted. 'I'm a doctor at Eastern Memorial Hospital. Can I assist in any way?'

The pharmacist looked relieved. 'I am trying to explain to Mrs Downer that any chest discomfort after having a pacemaker fitted should be looked at by a doctor. She wants some antacid but her symptoms may be masking something more serious.'

'Mrs Downer,' Matthew began, 'my name is Dr Harrison, and I agree with the pharmacist. You can't ignore chest problems after the surgery you have undergone. May I ask you a few questions?'

Breathlessly she answered, 'Yes, my dear. But my son Harold says it's just indigestion. He's in the car and he's in such a hurry to get me home tonight. He has an early flight in the morning and I really need to be there for Stanley.'

'Another few minutes here with us won't matter to either Harold or Stanley,' Matthew told her as he knelt down and took her pulse. 'Tell me, Mrs Downer, are you having any other symptoms?'

'I feel a little breathless and tight in the chest, but Harold says that's definitely indigestion.'

'Is Harold a doctor?'

Mrs Downer shook her head slightly. 'Goodness, no, dear. Harold is an architect.'

'Then perhaps Harold would be better leaving medical advice to others,' Matthew said politely as he looked up at the pharmacist, who was rolling his eyes in frustration. 'When did you have the pacemaker operation?'

'The day before yesterday. I had one night in hospital and then the doctor told me I could go home as I was doing so well. Harold needed me at home to take care of his cockatoo, Stanley, while he is away,' she said but her words became strained.

'Are you having any trouble swallowing?'

Mrs Downer nodded. 'Yes, and I feel a little dizzy too.'

'Please call for an ambulance, let them know suspected cardiac tamponade,' he told Beth in a low, calm voice to ensure he didn't alarm Mrs Downer. Turning his attention back to the elderly woman, he said, ' Mrs Downer, without tests I cannot be sure, but I believe you may be suffering a condition linked to the operation you had. You may have some fluid in the sac around your heart and we need to drain it off immediately.'

The woman seemed to be deteriorating by the minute.

'Do you have oxygen?' he asked the pharmacist.

Immediately the young man brought a cylinder and a mask to Beth, who placed it gently over the woman's face. 'Try to breathe normally,' she said in a reassuring tone.

It was only a few minutes before the siren of the ambulance was audible. And a minute later the paramedics arrived and carefully lifted Mrs Downer onto the barouche and strapped her in securely.

'I'll need you to start an IV and get her to Eastern Memorial. And can you call ahead and let them know we'll need a chest X-ray, twelve-lead ECG and an echocardiogram? We also need to type and cross-match a blood sample and check her potassium level.'

As they wheeled the elderly woman to the ambulance, a tall man, who looked to be in his late forties, appeared. 'What's all this, then? Where are you taking my mother?' he asked in an arrogant tone.

'Well, it's not indigestion, Harold, so she's going to hospital. I suspect she has a very serious condition related to her pacemaker. She has pressure building on her heart muscle, weakening its ability to pump. That happens when the pericardial space fills up with fluid faster than the pericardial sac can stretch—'

'And who are you to decide all this?' he cut in abruptly.

'Dr Matthew Harrison, A and E consultant at Eastern Memorial,' he replied curtly, as he changed the oxygen mask from the one given by the pharmacist to the one being held by the paramedics, and walked swiftly beside the barouche. 'If you want to follow in your car, please do so, but we are leaving now and I do not have time to go into any more detail about your mother's condition.'

With that, Matthew turned his attention away from the man and assisted the paramedics as they lifted the patient inside. Then he turned his attention to Beth.

'Are you okay to get back home?' he asked her. 'I don't like the idea of you walking alone at night.'

'I'll take the main road. I won't cut back through the park. I'll be fine, honestly. You go,' she told him, then added, 'But don't forget to take the codeine. You'll need it even more now.'

Matthew nodded and smiled briefly. 'Can you text me when you get home?'

Beth was surprised at his level of concern for her, not being accustomed to it. She had never had to check in with her family. They hadn't noticed when she'd been at home or out and had rarely asked where she had been. But she conceded it did feel nice to have someone look out for her.

'Certainly,' she answered him, barely swallowing a yawn. It had been a long day.

'I'll get a cab back to your place later to pick up my car,' he said, as he checked the patient's vitals. 'But please don't wait up.'

Matthew climbed in next to Mrs Downer and heard the second paramedic call ahead to the hospital with his instructions as the first paramedic shut the heavy doors then climbed on board and drove at top speed, with the siren wailing.

Beth watched as the ambulance disappeared down the street in the direction of the Eastern Memorial.

'That all seemed a little intense.'

Beth turned to see Harold watching the kerb where the ambulance had been.

'Seriously,' he added. 'Aren't they overreacting a bit? She's got indigestion. Old folks get it all the time.'

Beth couldn't believe what she was hearing. She had expected Harold to be tearing down the road in his car after the ambulance to be with his mother.

'No, Harold. It is most definitely not indigestion. Your mother has a potentially life-threatening condition.'

'You think?'

'I don't think, I know. Dr Harrison assessed your mother and he would not have requested an ambulance if it was not a serious condition. Dr Harrison does not overreact.' Beth thought how ironic this statement was, particularly coming from her. Matthew could definitely overreact. She had witnessed it first hand. But that was about his personal life, and his interns, and his rosters. But never about his patients, she conceded.

'Should I head in there, then?'

Beth raised an eyebrow and stared at the man in disbelief. 'I think you need to make that decision, Harold. But it might be nice for your mother if you gave her some empathy and support.' With that she walked away from Harold and headed to the crossing. As she waited for the lights to turn green, she turned back to see him rubbing his bald head and cursing loudly all the way back to his car.

'Charming,' she muttered under her breath.

Beth walked home alone but as she'd told Matthew she stayed on the main road until her street and then walked briskly to her door. It was a safe neighbourhood but she was aware it was late and dark. She unlocked her door, stepped inside and sent a text as he'd asked.

Ten minutes later the ambulance pulled into Emergency and Mrs Downer was immediately taken to X-ray.

'If my suspicions are confirmed, we'll need to prepare for a pericardiocentesis,' he told one of the attending nurses. 'Check that the cardiac consultant is available and, if not, secure at least a cardiac resident, stat.'

The nurse left Matthew and confirmed the consultant was available and on his way to A and E.

Matthew held Mrs Downer's hand as she was wheeled into X-ray. 'We just need some pictures to check your heart,' he told her as the nurses gently unbuttoned her blouse and prepared her for the X-ray and echocardiogram. 'You are in good hands now,' he said as he saw the cardiac consultant rush into A and E.

'Thanks, Matthew, I can take it from here. The paramedics filled me in,' the consultant said as he approached the patient. 'Great call by the sound of it.'

Matthew left the team working on the patient and headed out into the reception area to find Harold pacing the area, wringing his hands. After the polite rebuke from Beth he had driven to the hospital.

'Your mother is in X-ray and if I'm right she'll need to undergo a procedure to drain fluid from near her heart.'

'So someone didn't do their job properly two days ago, then?'

'I wouldn't go making accusations like that if I were you,' Matthew retorted. 'Sometimes patients develop problems after surgery. They are not in any way related to the level of care during procedure, it's the body's reaction afterwards.'

'Will she be staying overnight?'

'Your mother should be fine. She is in the best hands.' Matthew answered a question that Harold should have asked but hadn't.

'Will she be staying in, I asked.'

'Yes, she will most definitely be in hospital for a few days to monitor her condition.'

'Then I'll be off. I have an early flight tomorrow and I'll have to find someone else to take care of my bird now,' he explained as he turned to leave. As an afterthought he added, 'Let her know I'll call from Perth around lunchtime.' With that he was gone.

Matthew resisted his urge to follow Harold and tell him what a cold-hearted excuse for a son he was. He wasn't even waiting to find out the results of his mother's tests. It was bad enough that he had not taken her seriously after her procedure and had not even escorted her into the pharmacy, but now he was leaving her without waiting to check she was all right. It wasn't as if he was the pilot flying the plane and needed to be rested. He could sleep on the four-hour flight if need be.

Matthew didn't dislike birds, or any animals for that matter, but he did think Harold needed to reset his priorities and put his mother a little higher than his cockatoo.

Matthew rolled his aching shoulders as he looked at the text message from Beth. He debated whether to head to his office, despite it being after ten, or to get a cab to Beth's and pick up his car. His headache had subsided, thanks to the codeine.

He walked outside to hail a cab. The night air was still warm as he signalled for the next cab on the rank.

The trip was quick and for the first time in a very long time he closed his eyes and drifted off to sleep.

'We're here,' a voice called out loudly from the front of the cab.

Matthew woke up, unaware that it was the third time the driver had tried to wake him.

'I'm sorry, I must have drifted off. How much do I owe you?'

'Sixteen bucks…you can forget the twenty cents.'

Matthew reached for his wallet and handed the man a twenty. 'Please keep the change.'

He climbed out of the cab and saw that Beth's lights were still on. He wanted to spend more time with her. He didn't feel as if he had to keep the walls up. They were developing a friendship and he felt safe, something he hadn't felt in years.

He headed up to the front door. His finger hovered inches from the doorbell before his practical side kicked in. Just as quickly as he had reached her door he walked back down the path to his car. He couldn't do it. He had to leave. They were getting too close, even if it was in the guise of friendship. It was dangerously close to being more.

'Matthew?'

He turned and saw Beth standing in the doorway. She was wearing her summer pyjamas. It wasn't a negligee, it wasn't revealing or sexy. It was a T-shirt and boxer shorts with what looked like ducks printed on them. Her hair was tied loosely in an untidy ponytail high on her head.

'I just made some iced tea. It's still so awfully warm out. You're welcome to come in for a little while.'

Matthew felt he should say no. But around Beth he felt like he could be himself. And she seemed accepting of the idea of keeping it simple, keeping it platonic. Friendship seemed to be sitting comfortably with her. The problem was, he didn't know how it was really sitting with him.

'Are you sure?' he called back from the front gate, where he was standing with his hands in his trouser pockets.

'Of course. I asked, didn't I? But you'll have to excuse the outfit,' she said, looking down at her pyjamas. He had said not to wait up so she'd changed into her T-shirt and boxers and in her excitement to open the door had completely forgotten. She had heard the cab pull up and the door shut and had looked out of her window to see Matthew walk up to the door and then turn to leave so she'd rushed to get his attention. She wanted to spend more time with him. In any state of dress, she admitted to herself, pulling her hair loose from the sky-high messy do.

Matthew smiled, nodded and walked back up the path to the door and into Beth's home.

'Here it is,' she said, placing two tall glasses of iced tea on the coffee table in front of them. 'I have some more pavlova in the fridge if you'd—'

'Please, no more pavolva. Sit down before we both lapse into a sugar-induced coma.' Matthew gently grabbed Beth's wrist and pulled her onto the sofa beside him. The heat from his touch shot through her like electricity. She didn't want him to release her arm, she wanted him to touch more of her. All of her. She blinked as she looked at his handsome face so close. Close enough to kiss.

Matthew felt Beth's smooth skin under his fingers. It felt so good. Soft, warm…inviting. He released his hold. He didn't want to go down that road. They had set new parameters and he wanted to abide by them. For both their sakes.

He sat upright, shifting a little in his seat. 'Iced tea looks good,' he said, breaking the uncomfortable silence.

Beth steadied her emotions. She had to keep herself in check. She didn't want him to run away. Not again.

She reached for her glass and sipped the refreshing drink. 'How is your patient, Mrs Downer?' She knew she wasn't nervous around him any more. She had easily remembered the patient's name, unlike the first day at the hospital when she'd been a mess of nerves around him.

'Good. She's doing very well,' he replied. 'It was as I suspected, cardiac tamponade, and she'll be in Intensive Care overnight.'

'Great news and a great call,' she said, not trying to hide her admiration for his diagnostic skills. 'But I could have throttled her son. I'm not a violent person, but he's the lowest excuse for a human being. Not an ounce of sympathy for his poor mother.'

'Tell me about it,' Matthew agreed, resting back on the sofa. 'He left the hospital before the procedure to find a cockatoo sitter.'

'Now, there's a man with his priorities in place.' Beth shook her head with the absurdity of it all.

Matthew nodded and rolled his eyes in agreement.

He took another sip of his iced tea. It was refreshing and he felt relaxed. Beth was fun and warm and intelligent. But he felt he mustn't show her any sign of affection. That would lead to sex, which would ultimately lead to disaster for him.

He was grateful they had avoided any more discussion about his past. Being friends was easier than he'd first thought.

Beth wasn't sure how to raise an awkward

question, or indeed whether it was appropriate, but if they were to be friends she thought she ought to know more about Matthew's life. The good, the bad and the painful.

She coughed to clear her throat, wondering if this would be a bad time. But then she surmised no time would be a great time for Matthew to relive something that had crippled him emotionally for years. But as she had discussed her past, perhaps he would be able to do the same.

'Matthew, I know you said your fiancée left, and I don't mean to pry, but you writing off the idea of any future relationship makes me think there was something else you haven't told me.'

She swallowed again. Had she overstepped the mark?

Matthew closed his eyes and took a deep, controlled breath. He didn't say a word but Beth saw his jaw tensing. She realised she should have thought better than to ask such an intrusive question.

'I'm so sorry, I've gone and done it again,' she said, wishing her inquisitive nature would let things lie. 'Please just forget I asked.'

Matthew wished for a moment he had not cabbed it back or accepted Beth's invitation to come inside. He had hoped the sketchy details would suffice. The idea of going over the worst time in his life didn't sit comfortably with him, but then he realised Beth talking about her family could not have been a walk in the park either. He decided to tell her what he could. If it got too difficult, he planned on leaving. He knew where the door was and he could use it.

'I can tell you what happened if you really want to know, but you need to understand it won't make any difference.'

'Honestly, Matthew, you don't need to—'

'Maybe it will be better to talk about it. Get it out in the open.' He drew another deep breath and began. 'No one but my family knows. It was June five years ago. The tenth of June, to be exact. I wish I could forget the date but I can't. It's there, burned into my brain.'

Matthew got to his feet and crossed to the window, deep in thought. Beth knew this was hard on him so she didn't interrupt. She barely moved. He finally turned back and faced her. But he wasn't focusing on her, his gaze was nowhere in the room.

'Anne and I were driving home from a faculty dinner not far from Paddington, where we were living. It was raining, the usual Sydney winter weather. A car ran a red light and ploughed into the right-hand side of the car. I remember the impact, the car spinning and smashing into the Stobie pole. I looked over and saw that Anne had been thrown forward, but the airbag appeared to have protected her from serious damage. She was conscious. The airbags started deflating and I could see my legs were pinned in the buckled metal of the door but I couldn't feel any pain. I knew immediately I had damage not only to my legs but my spine.'

Beth gasped. 'Dear Lord, what happened?'

'After they cut me out of the wreck, I was transported to the Western Hills Hospital, where we both worked. My legs were both fractured, the right femur was smashed and the left tibia and fibula had multiple fractures. They also initially suspected category B traumatic spinal cord damage.'

'But that can't be. You'd be motor incomplete. You wouldn't be able to practise medicine.'

'I'm so grateful they were wrong. It turns out that I had mild incomplete injury at the T5 vertebrae. I spent months in Acute Care with physical therapists and occupational therapists.'

'And Anne wasn't injured?'

'A couple of bruises, at least that's what

they told me,' he said, crossing back to the armchair.

'Told you? You didn't see her?'

He sat on the edge of the armchair with his shoulders slouched a little. His breathing was strained. 'No, not after they cut me from the car. She apparently hightailed it out of the country when the attending physician told her his initial suspicions about the damage to my spine. She was a medico, she knew the prognosis was bad. Apparently nursing a cripple was not in her life plan. She didn't want to be my nurse and the breadwinner. That was five years ago.'

Beth was horrified to think a woman could walk out on a man like that. But it explained so much. The way Matthew kept people at a distance. The bursts of anger, the indifference to others' feelings at times, yet the glimpses of a loving man that lay deeper inside. He must have felt so abandoned, so betrayed.

She reached for his hands but he pulled away.

'When did you find out she had gone?'

'It was only a matter of days after the accident. I was still on morphine for the pain, and pretty groggy. I knew my prognosis wasn't good but even if I couldn't walk again I could still be involved in medicine, even if it was in a lecturing capacity. I was alive and I knew that we could get through it together. I remember asking the night-shift nurse where Anne was and she said she wasn't sure, but she had a strange pitying look on her face as she continued checking my obs. I started to worry Anne had suffered internal injuries and they were hiding it from me. It was the only explanation I could think of for her not visiting me. There was no other reason in my mind that she wouldn't be by my bedside.'

'Perhaps the nurse didn't know.'

'No, she knew.' He began shifting uncomfortably. 'Apparently it spread like wildfire around the hospital. It was like pity party central, I had so many visitors, but I kept asking for Anne.'

'Were your parents there for you?' she asked with concern etching her voice.

'Yes, they had flown down the day after the accident,' he said, wringing his hands.

'Did they know about your fiancée leaving?'

'My parents had met her leaving the hospital the night after the accident and she had told them she was leaving for Canada and gave them the engagement ring. They kept if from me for almost a week. Finally they had to tell me.

'I was gutted. I didn't know how to get from one day to the next. I had operations to face, I had physio, occupational therapy. I had the lot, and I had to deal with her leaving me on top of that.'

'That is so sad. I can't imagine anyone doing that, just walking away. It's so cold-hearted. I can't begin to know what you went through,' Beth said, tears welling in her eyes.

Matthew got to his feet again, and paced across the lounge. 'I don't want sympathy. I just need you to understand that's why I can't get involved. It's not you. It's me. She ripped my heart out. I don't have one to give to you, not any more.'

He was tired of hearing his voice and felt drained from reliving the nightmare. He couldn't continue. He had already told her more than she needed to know and much more than he had ever expected to tell anyone.

Beth suddenly felt like she knew the man before her. She could only imagine Matthew lying in hospital, not knowing if he would ever walk again, let alone if he could practise medicine, and then reaching out to find that the woman he loved had walked away.

The woman with whom he had planned to spend his life had turned her back on him. The emptiness, shock and disappointment must have been overwhelming. Beth was surprised that she had got as close as she had to Matthew before he'd shut the relationship down.

He looked at her and knew from her expression and the tears on her cheek that she understood.

'Please, don't feel sorry for me. I want more than anything to be friends. If you can accept that, I will be a happy man for the first time in a very long time.' He sat down beside her and waited for her answer.

Beth had no choice. She loved him, and she suspected he knew it. But that wasn't to be. She had to accept it.

'Friends,' she said, wiping away the traces of the tears still clinging to her face. 'Best friends.' She rested her head on the shoulder of the man she loved with all her heart.

CHAPTER EIGHT

IT HAD BEEN over a week since the night Beth and Matthew had opened up to each other about their pasts. Beth had accepted friendship was the limit of their relationship. She was sad that Matthew couldn't move on from the hurt, but she valued him in her life so she didn't ask for more than he could give her. Matthew had found a friend in Beth like no other. She was the most amazing woman and he felt fortunate to have her in his life.

Working together was easy and the entire A and E team sensed a difference. The team dynamics were positive and Matthew looked forward to work, not as an escape but an opportunity to spend more time with Beth.

It was Monday morning and Emergency was frantic with the arrival of victims of a crash on the freeway involving a tourist bus, three cars and a delivery van. The passengers from the cars and the driver of the van had arrived first.

Dan was working flat out, tending to those with back injuries.

'It's like a war zone today,' he commented, as he passed Beth rushing back to another bay where the next patient had been wheeled in.

Beth just nodded and collected the next barouche as it arrived from yet another ambulance.

'Did they call ahead with the number of patients?' she asked, concern in her voice. They had called all the available residents from the wards to A and E to handle the patient load and they were still struggling.

'I think the final tally will be over twenty-five and I just heard the tourist bus has a few heading in with little or no English.'

'That will be a challenge,' she remarked, as she obtained IV access and asked the nurse to hook up a drip with morphine for her patient with a suspected thoracic spine injury. She ordered a portable X-ray and left that patient for a moment. Throwing her gloves away, she slipped on a new pair and engaged with the next victim lying on a barouche in the corridor. She looked in her early twenties and her jaw was bloodied, with splinters of glass embedded in the tissue. Beth wasn't sure if she had been thrown through the windshield or if something had pushed the windshield into the car and her face. As she worked at carefully removing the glass fragments she suspected temporomandibular injuries. She asked the nurse to call down the oral surgery consultant and had the patient hooked up to IV pain relief.

The patients were wheeled into the bays in quick succession, residents working alongside consultants to tend to the injured and move them into wards or operating theatres. Beth thought back to Dan's description of a battle zone and as she looked around her she couldn't help but agree. There were barouches everywhere and, although all were being monitored by the additional nursing staff, it was at times almost overwhelming. Interpreters assisted the non-English-speaking tourists when they arrived, but overwhelmed by the medical trauma they were witnessing the interpreters became anxious and added to the stress of the situation.

A small number of patients were treated and allowed to leave but they were asked to see their general practitioners as it was explained to them that after serious car accidents those affected could suffer short- or long-term psychological effects and could develop conditions that closely resembled post-traumatic stress disorder.

It was almost eleven that night before all the patients had been treated and admitted or released from the hospital. It had been a marathon of a day. Beth was close to exhaustion but in a strange way she had enjoyed the pace, the adrenalin rush and the satisfaction of seeing positive outcomes for the patients. They hadn't lost a single life, and it could have been very different.

She could not help but admire Matthew's ability to work under pressure, making life-and-death decisions without flinching. He was an amazing doctor and a brilliant leader. She was trying to look at him in a different light. She wouldn't let herself think of him romantically but instead as a mentor. He guided everyone to ensure that the patients survived potentially fatal injuries. He was the best at what he did and Beth admired and respected him. She still wished there could be more to their relationship but accepted that she was fortunate to have a year at the hospital learning from such an amazing doctor.

'I think we all need to get home,' Matthew said to Dan and Beth as he passed them in the corridor, slipping off his coat and taking a deep breath. It was his first moment to stop in a very long day.

'No argument from me,' Dan remarked. 'I could sleep for a few days after that shift.'

'Are you rostered on tomorrow?'

'I am,' Dan replied with a smile, 'but I will sleep like a log tonight and be fighting fit tomorrow.'

'Before you go, Dan,' Matthew continued, 'I want to let you know that you both did a great job today. In fact, the entire week. You worked under pressure and you made well-informed calls and the teamwork was second to none. Proud to have you both in A and E.'

Dan stood open-mouthed for a moment. He couldn't believe the praise that Matthew had just bestowed on them both. Dan admired Matthew immeasurably but he had become accustomed to his barking.

Finally he mustered some words, 'Thank you, Dr Harrison. I enjoy being a part of A and E.' With that he gave a light-hearted salute and made his way to the doctors' lounge to collect his gear before heading home.

Matthew turned his attention to Beth. 'You should be very happy with today, Beth.'

'I am, but we have a great mentor so that does make it easier.'

Matthew smiled. 'I can drop you home, if you'd like.'

Beth nodded. 'That would be wonderful. I'm not too keen taking a cab this late. I worry I'll fall asleep on the way home.'

'I'll get my things from my office while you get changed—I'll be about ten minutes.' With that Matthew headed to his office and Beth went to get changed and grab her bag. It was hot outside so she quickly jumped into the shower in the locker room and then changed into a dress she had left in her locker in case she decided to go shopping or catch a bite to eat after work one night. She felt like a bedraggled mess after so many hours working on her feet and the shower made her feel human again.

It was only a few minutes before they both emerged and made their way to the car park.

Matthew smiled as he looked at his passenger. He was still guarding his heart and wasn't sure if it would ever be whole enough to offer to her, but she made him feel good about the future. While he doubted they would be more than friends, deep inside his heart said, *Never say never.*

The drive home was quick as there were few cars on the road at that time of the night.

'Would you like that proper English cup of

tea I promised you a week ago?' Beth asked as she stifled a yawn.

Matthew wanted to spend a little more time with her, even though he knew she was tired. He had spent far too much time at work or alone over the last few years and he was revelling in having someone special in his life. Someone with whom he could share his day and talk about the crazy world of A and E, knowing she understood and felt the same about it. The challenges, the sadness, the frustration and elation they experienced every day.

'I accept…but only one cup and I'll be gone. Can't have you collapsing from exhaustion.'

Beth put the kettle on as soon as they were inside and Matthew made himself comfortable on the sofa after Beth told him the kitchen was too small for two of them and she didn't need his help. It wasn't long before she emerged with a tray holding a pot of tea, complete with tea cosy, two teacups, milk and sugar. She let the tea brew for a few minutes and then poured them both a cup, adding milk.

Beth rested back on the sofa, curling her feet under her legs, and sipped the tea as if it were as precious as liquid gold. Matthew sipped his tea and watched her face as she closed her eyes with each sip. He was sympathetic about how tired she would be feeling so he finished his cup and then bade her goodnight. With her shoes kicked off onto the floor, she walked barefoot to the door to say goodnight. She reached up to kiss him on the cheek but he suddenly pulled her into his arms. It seemed so right to hold her. Beth didn't move away. She wanted to feel him next to her. Suddenly his reservations disappeared. They melted away in the warmth of her touch, her skin, her body.

Despite the day they had endured and the exhaustion they both had felt only moments ago, they didn't want to pull away from each other. They wanted to feel the warmth and the closeness. He had been so alone and so lonely for so long. He had his arms around a woman who had become his best friend. A woman he now had to admit he desired beyond his control.

Without warning, they became two people tired of fighting the need to be with each other.

She felt protected by his arms wrapped around her body. He made her feel vulnerable to him yet safe from the world. She looked up into the eyes of the man holding her so tightly. He was the man of her dreams. He was the one.

She felt her breasts crushed against his chest as he held her possessively. He kissed her softly until gentleness surrendered to passion and his lips parted hers with urgency. His hands caressed the bare skin of her arms and as he tenderly undid the bow of her halter dress, letting the ties fall across her bare shoulders. Suddenly his patience departed and he unzipped the back of her dress and discarded it in one swift move.

'I don't want to stop,' he breathed huskily as his mouth moved low on her neck. 'I want to make love to you.'

She nodded as she felt his teeth pulling gently on her small hoop earrings and his tongue lightly teasing her skin. Beth was silenced by her desire for this man. He was releasing in her an unrestrained need she had never dreamed possible. Although she couldn't tell him—not now, at least—she loved him with all her heart.

Her fingers moved freely over his chest and as if he had read her mind, his hands met hers and together they slid his T-shirt over his head. The taut muscles beneath were inviting her touch and there was no hesitation from Beth as she eagerly explored his smooth skin. His kisses deepened and she met his need with her hunger. Her hands slipped up to his neck, and ran through the dark locks of his hair, pulling his lips down harder on hers.

But then without warning his firm hands reached up and closed around her wrists, halting their sensual foray.

'I suggest we move to a more comfortable location…'

Beth stood before Matthew with only her strapless bra and cream lace panties covering her body. He pulled her back into his arms so their bodies moulded tightly together. This close, Beth was mindful of his raw masculinity and the effect he was having on her equilibrium. At this moment he was no longer her superior or mentor. Matthew Harrison was moments from being her lover. Taking his hand, Beth led him to her bedroom. She didn't switch on any lights, letting the lamp in the lounge provide a soft glow to the room. Despite their long day, it would be an even longer night of lovemaking.

Morning came and Beth wanted to savour each precious moment after she woke. They had both fallen into a deep sleep in the early hours of the morning. It felt so good to be wrapped in Matthew's arms. He had been more passionate than she had ever imagined. Underneath the hurt and distrust was a loving man. And a man who knew how to make love in a way she had never thought possible. He had made her feel like the only woman in the world. The earth hadn't just moved, it had shaken and trembled and quaked.

Beth had known she was in love before she'd taken him to her bed. She hoped his heart was heading in the same direction.

She could hear the phone ringing in her bag in the lounge and she quickly but carefully slid out the bed. Mindful that Matthew hadn't woken up, she closed the bedroom door. She felt a little self-conscious naked in the morning light so she grabbed her dress from the floor and stepped into it.

'Hello,' she said softly, trying not to wake Matthew.

'Hello, petal,' came her father's voice. 'How are you?'

She was surprised to hear his voice and even more surprised to hear him call her 'petal'. He hadn't called her that in years. 'I'm fine, Father. How are you?'

'Not wonderful. I've made the decision to leave Hattie. And not a moment too soon.'

Beth sat down on a patio chair in stunned silence for a moment. She hadn't heard a word from him since she'd left for Australia and now he was calling to break this news. 'What happened?'

'I haven't been happy for years but the final straw came when Hattie booked the Ritz Carlton for Charlotte's wedding reception. I can't be the bottomless purse for those two any more.'

'Charlotte's getting married?'

'Yes, she met a young man at one of her events and they are planning on marrying just before Christmas. It's been years of putting up with their demands and I won't do it any more. This was the final straw. I've had it with the pair of them.'

Beth listened intently as her father described his disappointment with his marriage to Hattie. 'I thought that Hattie could fill the void in my heart after your mother died. But she couldn't. I was scared of being alone and I rushed into the relationship. She ran hot and cold. One minute I was the man of her dreams and then next I was the devil incarnate.'

'She definitely had her moments,' Beth agreed. 'But I am sure she loved you in her own way.' Beth was trying to console her father. She wasn't sure why but she felt the need to soften the blow and try to show Hattie in a positive light. Perhaps it was to protect her father from the fact that Hattie was, in her mind, a gold-digger. She had liked spending George's money. She'd enjoyed the social standing, the parties, the dinners, the lifestyle that marrying a man like George had accorded her—rather than George the man himself, Beth suspected.

'Perhaps, but I'm filing for divorce. The matter is with my attorney now. My blood pressure is through the roof and I was hoping you could come home and we could go on a trip together. Maybe abroad. I would love to see the Amalfi Coast.'

'Now?' Her father had not needed her for the best part of eighteen years and now he needed her.

'My cardiologist says unless I get my blood pressure down I'm looking at a bypass. I know it's a lot to ask of you, but I really need you, Beth. I took the liberty of speaking with Edward Lancaster last night and he has agreed to give you an indefinite leave of absence from the Eastern Memorial, starting as soon as you like. Professor Rowe gave me his details.' He paused for a moment. 'All we have is each other.'

Those words stabbed right through Beth's heart. She had waited so long for her father to pay her the attention she had enjoyed as a little girl and now he needed her.

She looked back towards the house and her bedroom. Matthew was there. He was in her bed, waiting for her. But she also knew she couldn't turn her back on her father.

She knew what she had to do. Her father needed her. But she had finally found someone who she thought could be her future. A man who might possibly make her the centre of his world. Why was life so unfair? she wondered.

Her father would not go abroad without her. She couldn't risk him staying in a stressful situation. She had to go and hope that Matthew would understand. She would only be gone a month or two and she would make it up to him when she got back.

'Is there anything keeping you there?' her father asked.

'No, I can be there by the end of the week. You have already made the arrangements with the hospital here, so it's done.'

'I knew you wouldn't let me down. I'll get on to my travel agent and have her email you the flight details. It's my shout. See you soon, petal.'

'Bye, Father.' With that she hung up and sat back, wondering how her life had just been turned upside down without warning. Hattie had managed to ruin Beth's childhood and teenage years and now it appeared the timing of her departure from their lives was going to affect her love life. But only short term, Beth reminded herself.

Beth had not heard Matthew get up and come out to the patio. He was leaning on the doorframe, smiling at the woman who he felt sure would be his future.

It had taken him five long years to heal and find a woman to trust. A woman who he knew would never leave him. Before Beth had came into his life, he had resigned himself to being alone, believing he would never find love again. And yet here he was, standing on her patio after an amazing night together, thinking about having her back in his arms as soon as possible. And if he had anything to do with it, they would not be getting out of bed any time soon. Life just didn't get any better. In his mind he knew he had found his soulmate. He was ready to think about love again.

He stepped closer and noticed she looked distracted. 'Is anything wrong?'

She looked up at to see Matthew wrapped in a white towel hung low on his hips. He was gorgeous, even more gorgeous in the morning light. She couldn't believe she was about to leave him to head back to England. Even though it was only for a month or two, she hated the universe at that moment for the timing of her father's divorce.

'Just my father,' she began as she lifted her feet onto the seat and cradled her ankles. She didn't want to spoil the mood but she had to tell him. She bit her lip and hoped he would understand.

'Is everything all right?'

'I have to return to London.'

Matthew stepped away from her. It was instinct. He recoiled from her words. 'Why?'

'He needs me home, he's not well and he needs to get away.'

'And when is this happening?'

'Apparently Dr Lancaster has approved it, effective immediately, so by the end of the week.' She didn't want to leave but she didn't see she had any choice.

'You can't be serious about leaving with a minute's notice,' Matthew retorted in disbelief.

Beth stood up and walked towards Matthew. 'I'm totally serious. My father needs me back home. Stress has elevated his blood pressure. He needs to get away from everything and he wants me with him. He's making the travel arrangements as we speak. But I'll be back here in a month or two.'

'A month or two?' he muttered, taken aback by the matter-of-fact delivery of the news. 'Or maybe not at all.'

'I will be back, you have to believe me, but it's important for me to go now. He needs me.'

'A flight to his bedside I would get. But a trip home to take a nice holiday doesn't sound like an emergency.'

Matthew wasn't buying Beth's story. After all, she had told him about her family so he couldn't understand her leaving so abruptly to support a man who had not been there for her. It was an excuse. He suspected she wanted out and was using her father to get away.

'Don't hide behind your father. Just say you want to go and be done with it.'

To Matthew it made no sense. Only a few hours ago they had been making love and now she was planning on leaving. Unable to think clearly, he stormed back to the bedroom and began gathering his things. He was reliving his nightmare. The woman who he had held in his arms and made love to all night was leaving him without a word. And without a moment's hesitation. She had made a quick and cold-hearted decision to leave. To fly halfway around the world with no return date, with as much thought as if she was going to the corner store. Clearly their relationship meant nothing to her. He had risked everything emotionally and she was being so casual. So cold.

'Matthew, wait,' Beth called after him. 'I need to explain.'

Matthew had already returned to the bedroom and begun dressing.

Beth rushed after him. 'I need to do this for him,' she said as she watched Matthew do up the last button on his shirt in silence. Beth wasn't sure that was the truth. She suspected she needed her father more than he would ever need her. This was an opportunity to be his sole focus, if only for a short time.

Matthew was crushed. He was being left again. He had opened his heart and Beth was walking all over it. His judgement of women, he realised, was worthless. He had finally given in to his heart and his feelings for this woman and immediately she wanted a couple of months away. He doubted that she would return. And he knew even if she did, his trust never would. She could up and leave any time. This proved it.

He reached for his wallet on the dresser without saying a word.

'I know my timing is terrible and how you must be feeling—'

'You have no idea what I'm feeling,' Matthew cut in angrily.

'But I have no choice.'

Matthew closed his eyes. 'You have every choice, Beth. You have the choice to say no to your father. To tell him to take his wife or his stepdaughter. But you won't. You want to take the scraps of attention he's finally throwing at you. Well, I won't do the same.'

Beth understood what Matthew was saying, but she had been hurting for a long time too. She needed to see if being away from England for even the shortest time had made her father miss her. Could she be a priority in his life again?

'He doesn't have anyone but me. He's left Hattie. He's filing for divorce.'

'Well, lucky you. If he still had her, I wonder if he would have made the call.'

Beth was taken aback by his comment. She didn't want to admit that she felt there was truth to what he said. *Would her father have called if he'd still had Hattie in his life?* She swallowed hard and pushed that thought away.

'He's been busy and now he realises that we need time together.'

'Stop it right there,' he snarled, as he made his way to the front door. 'You are heading back to the man who has ignored you for God knows how many years. I'm not your keeper but I thought you might give me some consideration before making such a decision. I would never have said you shouldn't go to him, it's not my place. But you pretended you wanted to be in a relationship and yet you didn't even talk to me about it. People in real relationships discuss things like this. They don't run off without warning.'

'But my father isn't well—'

'A holiday for high blood pressure is not an emergency that needs to have him pull strings at the hospital. He didn't even wait to see if you wanted to go before he made the call to Lancaster.'

'He was desperate to have me back home.'

'He had you for twenty-eight years. I've had you in my life for two weeks. Don't I deserve a bit more time to see where this might go?'

'I'll be back in a few months,' she implored, tears welling in her eyes.

'Wonderful,' he said, trying to hold together the last tenuous threads of his emotions. 'Don't bother giving me your return date, I won't be waiting. You obviously see this as a one-night stand. The rules for that are clear: one night, no obligations, no commitment.'

Beth could hardly believe her ears. Matthew was behaving irrationally. She was leaving for a few months to help her father.

Matthew was hurting more than he had thought possible. It wasn't his pride, although that had been ripped apart too. This was more. He had let Beth in and now he had to shut her out.

That was a lingering pain that he wouldn't inflict on himself. Not again.

'You chose to make plans as though there was nothing to keep you here. Turns out you're right. There's nothing here for you so just go.' Matthew picked up his keys from the hallstand and turned to face Beth. He felt like he was breaking and he couldn't stay even a moment longer and risk her seeing it. He turned away abruptly. He had to get out of the house and away from Beth.

He was fuming all the way home. He was surprised he didn't write the car off on the way. It took all his focus not to find the first bar and drink himself into oblivion. His fiancée had almost destroyed him and now the universe had sent Beth to finish the job.

Opening the door to his apartment and throwing his keys across the floor, he made a vow to never allow a woman to get close to him again. He felt like he was on the precipice and he had to hold himself together. He was not about to let another woman pull him into a dark place. He stepped into the shower and the steaming water hit his body. The memories of the previous night came rushing at him. He sneered at the fact that only a few hours ago he had actually thought he was the luckiest man alive.

He turned in the shower and the hot water ran over his face. He had to steel himself not to remember how the last two weeks had made him feel whole again. And last night he had discovered that underneath Beth's consultant's coat was a woman who wanted to be loved and knew how to please a man. He ran his fingers through his wet hair and turned the water to cold and then off. He leant against the tiles and took deep purposeful breaths. He had to harden himself against this woman. Against every woman. He was not going to break.

Matthew changed his clothes and decided to head into work. He was rostered off but there was always paperwork and he needed a distraction. Work. A familiar, reliable distraction. His only companion for the last five years.

Ten minutes later Matthew was on his way to the hospital, a different man. He was no longer a man in love. Matthew was going to harden his heart like never before. As he travelled through the early morning traffic, he tried to drive Beth from his mind. He fought the images of her beautiful face and her body lying naked on the bed. He had thought she was perfect in every way. But clearly she didn't feel the same. If she had felt the same she wouldn't be able to just leave. He changed gears so brutally he almost left the gearbox on the road.

Beth dressed quickly after Matthew left and stepped outside for a walk to clear her head. She wondered if she had made a mistake. Had she agreed too quickly to return to England? Was Matthew right to question the sense in her running back to a man who had ignored her for longer than she could remember? She didn't know how long she would walk but she didn't want to go home. She had so much to sort in her head.

Hours later, she was still walking and her

head hurt from the assault of her thoughts. She knew what she needed to do, and that was to go to her father. She knew what she *wanted* to do, and that was to stay with Matthew. But her conscience ruled her heart. She had to go back home. The decision was made.

She was on the afternoon shift. She had tried calling Matthew but it rang out. He had switched off his message bank so she couldn't even leave a message. But, then, what was the point? she wondered. She was leaving. There was nothing she could say. No other way to put it. He needed to accept it.

She finally made it home and closed the door behind her. Matthew's scent was still in the air. Beth wanted to rewind her life. To be lying in Matthew's arms. To be kissing his soft mouth, feeling his body next to hers. But she couldn't. He had gone.

CHAPTER NINE

MATTHEW STORMED INTO A and E and demanded to know why there were so many people in the waiting room.

'It's been chaos this morning,' Yvette told him. 'Dan, Will and two other residents from cardio and ENT have been working nonstop.'

'Well, clearly they need to work more efficiently. Or maybe we need to look at replacing them,' he announced as he grabbed a file and called for the next patient.

Dan appeared from behind the curtain of the bay where he had been treating a woman with suspected appendicitis. 'Yvette, please get a surgical resident down here now. Let them know we've got pain, anorexia, leukocytosis, and fever so they need to be prepped in OR for an emergency appendectomy.'

Yvette nodded and made the call and within minutes the surgical consultant arrived with a resident in tow. They examined the patient and agreed with Dan's diagnosis and took the patient straight to Theatre.

'What a morning,' he sighed as he approached the reception desk. 'I could do with a break.'

'Then you're in the wrong line of work. I don't need anyone around here who isn't up to the job,' Matthew yelled at the young resident, out of earshot of the patients.

'I was just saying—'

'That you needed a rest,' he cut in. 'Holidays are the time for resting. Not while you are on duty. And if I'm not mistaken you had some time off recently so I guess you're out of luck with that.' Matthew handed Dan the next patient's notes. 'If I were you I'd be back to work before your place is filled by someone more dedicated. There's a long list of young doctors who'd kill for this placement.' With that he told Yvette to call X-Ray as his patient had swallowed a small metal object and he wanted to ensure it had actually been swallowed and not inhaled and lodged in her lungs.

Dan stood speechless with the case notes in his hand, watching Matthew disappear into one of the bays. 'What the hell just happened?' he asked finally. 'Hannibal has returned. Where's the sensitive dude who actually liked me yesterday? I want *him* back.'

'Dan,' came the voice from the bay, 'are you still at Reception?'

'No, just bringing the next patient in now,' Dan replied, then motioned for the elderly patient to follow him.

The tone of the day was set. Matthew was unrelenting in his demands of all his staff. They were all in shock and dismayed at his change of demeanour.

A and E was busy when Beth arrived for the afternoon shift. She quickly changed and went to greet Yvette at Reception but it was her rostered day off and Vivian was there with a new nurse.

'Morning, Beth,' Vivian said cheerily, as she had only just clocked on and had not yet witnessed Matthew's foul temper. 'Hope you had a good morning off.'

'Not too bad,' Beth lied. 'Looks like another full house today.'

'Been steady since about six this morning apparently,' Vivian said. 'Beth, I'm not sure if you've met Alli, she's our new nurse. Just started today.'

Beth went to open her mouth when Matthew appeared.

'If you can stop chatting and process the

patients, we might actually save a few lives today,' he barked at the three of them. His glare stayed on Beth the longest.

'I was just introducing Alli,' Vivan explained in a low voice.

'I am sure that Alli is perfectly capable of introducing herself to everyone and assisting with patients.'

Beth looked at Matthew, hoping to see a glimpse of the man she had fallen in love with, but instead she saw a cold, blank stare. There was nothing there that looked like he felt any emotion towards her. Absolutely nothing. She needed to sort this out in the privacy of his office later. She hoped he would see reason if she could sit him down and just explain but until then she would go about her work. Her dirty laundry did not need a public airing.

'I'd better get started,' Beth announced casually.

'In regard to that,' Matthew retorted, 'I would prefer that you do not see any critical cases until further notice.' Then, turning to Vivian and Alli, he remarked, 'Anything critical will be given to Dan, Will or the other residents assigned to A and E today.'

Matthew knew Beth was competent but by reassigning her the less critical cases he knew he would not have to spend time with her. He would see her in passing but that was all. She would be down at the far end of A and E and they would definitely not be working on patients together. Being close to this woman even in a professional capacity was more than he could bear.

Beth couldn't believe what she was hearing. This reduced responsibility was a blatant attempt to punish her because she hadn't consulted him about her need to return to England. She had to sort this out sooner rather than later.

'As you wish,' she said. 'But I would like to speak with you today in your office.'

'I will check my schedule and get back to you,' he replied coldly.

The day was impossibly slow and boring for Beth. She started with a patient suffering an infected ingrown toenail and another with measles. Matthew had made it clear to both Vivian and Alli that he would not tolerate any challenge of his decision. Beth was only to handle the less critical cases. Both were confused but followed his directive. They were not about to rile the beast further. The day of treating minor cuts, abrasions and sprains finished with Beth still nursing a headache from hell and an acute case of boredom.

She hoped, given time, Matthew would see reason. He had to. She didn't see it as the end of them. Just a short break. She knew in her heart she would be back. He just needed to know that too.

She was standing at the Reception desk, waiting for one of her final female patients for the day to return from the bathroom with a specimen. She suspected honeymoon cystitis but needed confirmation from the lab.

'I for one would like you to patch it up,' Dan began, as he grabbed the next file from the larger than normal pile. 'Hannibal has been on the rampage since first thing this morning. I will need long-term therapy if this continues. He was near on impossible to please for the first six months of my residency, pleasant for almost two weeks, and yesterday—well, he was close to a saint… And now it's the return of the dictator. Clearly you are the reason for the personality disorder, so please just sort it out. Whatever it takes, and I mean whatever it takes. We are all living on our nerves around him and we'll all be thrown out of the hospital for self-medicating if this keeps up.'

'I wish I could, Dan, for all of us. But it's not in my power,' she answered curtly. 'Besides, you are getting the challenging cases and I've been relegated those needing sticking plasters, so why are you complaining?'

'I've noticed you're getting the boring stuff today. But we're all in the firing line again and the atmosphere around here is toxic.' Dan stopped in his tracks and grabbed Beth lightly by her shoulders. 'All I'm saying is whatever you did before made Harrison a contender for world's greatest boss. Think back and just do it again.'

Beth shook free and took the file from Vivian. 'Dr Harrison has his own issues and that is all I can say on the matter.'

Beth wasn't about to tell Dan what had happened. He could just go on thinking that Matthew was an irritable son of a bitch and leave it at that. He wasn't going to know about the night Beth had shared with him. She turned her attention from Dan to Vivian. 'What do we have here?' she asked, looking over the file notes.

'A rusty nail in the heel. Went through the patient's boot in the garden. The nail's gone and there's no bleeding, but he'll need a tetanus booster.'

Beth rolled her eyes. 'Now, that's going to be a stretch for me to handle,' she remarked. 'Shall I ask for back-up?' She turned and called across the waiting room, 'Mr Oliver?'

A middle-aged man stood and limped across the room and followed her into a bay, where she took his vitals and administered the tetanus booster.

Beth found the rest of the evening to be as mundane. Matthew was critical and demanding of everyone around. He refused to make a time to talk. His door was closed when he was in there and Beth had a steady stream of minor medical complaints to keep her too busy to go and search for him.

'Are you going to completely freeze me out?' she demanded of him when she finally confronted him as he was leaving Reception.

Matthew ignored her question and kept walking until he was almost at his office door. 'Aren't you off to England in a day or so, Dr Seymour? I don't seem to have any paperwork on my desk.'

'My father's travel agent is sending through the details tomorrow. Please, Matthew, can't we talk about it? This is ridiculous.'

'Ridiculous was me thinking that you wanted a relationship.'

'We can make it work. I love you—'

'Don't,' he answered, trying not to feel anything for the woman standing so close to him. He was so angry. He had never imagined when he'd lain in her bed that she could bring all the pain he had buried to the surface again. He just wanted her to go away. He wanted to shut her out of his mind and his heart. Forget he'd ever met her. Forget that he had started to fall in love with her. He had to tell himself it had never happened and go back to life the way it had been.

'Don't say another word. Just be honest. Tell it like it is, it was a one-night stand. Pleasant enough but short-lived. Nothing more, let's both move on and leave it at that.'

Beth felt sick to hear him talk this way. In her mind it had been so far from a one-night stand, but her life was complicated and he needed to understand. 'It was so much more than that and you know it.'

Matthew stormed back down the corridor to Beth like a man possessed. 'I walked out to see you on the patio this morning,' he said barely holding his emotions in tact. 'And you drop the bombshell you're heading to the other side of the world, without even bothering to see what I think about the idea? It was as if as soon as we'd slept together it was over. You couldn't wait to wipe your hands of me.'

Beth cringed at the way Matthew had made it sound.

'My feelings are real and still the same today as yesterday.'

'Maybe they weren't real yesterday either.' The blood was pumping hard in his chest. 'Don't worry, I'm over it.'

He walked inside his office and began to close the door on Beth.

'Well, clearly you're not over it,' she retorted. 'You're punishing me. Limiting my patient load to minor abrasions is stupid and childish.'

Matthew had never wanted to punish Beth. He was angry because he loved her. And he was painfully aware that was his problem, not Beth's. He couldn't be around her knowing she was able to walk away so easily, not sure when or perhaps even if she would return.

'Then do us both a favour and leave, Dr Seymour.'

The door slammed shut.

Beth was so angry and so sad. She was sorry for the way it had happened. She wasn't sure if she could have handled it any better. If she had left it longer to tell Matthew, he would have no doubt accused her of hiding her plans. It was a lose-lose situation for her. Clearly Matthew would never have accepted her leaving. He just didn't understand.

Finally being important to her father, being needed by him, it was like a dream come true for Beth. She just hoped it would last. She hoped her return to England would be worth the price Matthew was making her pay.

He had only until the end of the week until she left. Three long days. The best she could hope for was a truce. She hoped to return to her position at the Eastern when she came back from London. Maybe, given time, and working together again, Matthew would come to his senses. He would see the trip for what it was. Nothing more. And they could pick up the pieces. She hoped for that with all of her heart.

Beth wanted things to be civil between them so she accepted his decision to limit her to minor cases. She treated each patient with the same care and respect as she would a critical patient but the day was routine and she knew that her skills could be better utilised. She could take the pressure off the others and let them have the occasional non-urgent patient, but Matthew had not let it happen.

Beth had fallen asleep on the couch in her sitting room after arriving home and completely missed the alarm clock ringing in the bedroom the next morning.

Her make-up was sparse and hurried, but it didn't concern her, and her examination coat was covering her indifferent choice of taupe trousers and a cream knitted top. As she passed beneath the cool breeze from the air-conditioning vent inside the doors of the hospital she could feel the dampness in her plaited hair. She had washed it and literally run out of the door.

Beth arrived for the morning shift to find A and E was chaotic. Two ambulances were in the bay, with paramedics unloading barouches, and three more were still en route. Matthew was nowhere to be found, so Beth took herself off restricted duty. She suspected her relegation was only going to be for a day anyway. Once he had cooled off, Beth assumed Matthew would allow her to return to her normal duties.

Yvette filled her in on the details as she scrubbed, gloved and slipped on protective glasses. Scaffolding had collapsed outside a city hotel, injuring not only two workers but also the pedestrians caught underneath.

While one barouche was hurriedly wheeled into the examination room of the surgical resident, another was pushed into Beth's examination bay, with a paramedic astride the patient. He was applying direct pressure to an injured leg, which had been elevated slightly. The paramedic informed her that the patient was one of the workers. He had fallen two stories and impaled his upper leg on a metal support beam, but the beam had collapsed with his weight and fallen further, releasing him onto the pavement.

A saline drip had been connected and he had been administered intravenous morphine, but with the immense blood loss he had lost consciousness.

The paramedic released his weight and Beth expeditiously cut away the pressure bandage.

'Cross-match for three units, but we'll start with plasma substitute. I need a portable X-ray,' Beth said urgently, and called for his vital signs as Yvette hooked up the brownish emergency solution to the stand.

'Seventy over fifty… Sixty over forty… Fifty over forty…'

Beth knew immediately he had severed an artery as the pulsing blood loss matched his heartbeat. She suspected it may be his femoral artery, but in the bloodied mess of ripped tissue it was difficult to see.

'Suction!' she called. 'He's losing blood too fast.'

The floor around the barouche was flooded with the man's blood.

'I want a Spencer Wells clamp in here and I need more light,' Beth said to the nurse as she struggled to control the pumping vessel in the gaping wound. As she leaned closer to examine the injuries, splashes of blood hit the plastic lenses of her glasses. Anxiously, she patted at them with her sleeve before the young nurse wiped away the blood with gauze.

Finally Beth managed to reach one of the severed arteries and slow the bleeding and the man's blood pressure stabilised. But she knew there was deeper damage.

'Forget X-ray, Yvette, call OR. I want this man taken up there now.'

Beth monitored the open wound, leaving the clamp in position and maintaining direct pressure, as she waited for the surgical team to retrieve the man. The minutes seemed to pass with disturbing delay before the gowned orderlies and a surgical resident rushed through and sped the barouche into emergency surgery. It was up to the surgical team now, since she had done all she could. He had lost a lot of blood but unless there were other serious internal injuries, Beth felt confident he would survive.

She scrubbed, re-gowned and saw two more victims of the horrendous accident in quick succession. Thankfully neither was as serious and despite both needing hospitalisation for fractures and concussion, their prognoses were good.

Beth had just sat down to complete the last patient's notes before transfer when Matthew stormed into the room. He had heard Beth was treating critical injuries. While he knew she was more than competent to tend to the patients' injuries, he didn't want to have to work alongside her. He wanted to keep her at arm's length and once again feel safe. Backed up against the wall, he chose to exhibit his anger and mask any feelings he still had for her.

'Why didn't you call for back-up?' he bellowed.

It was clear his anger hadn't abated. Beth had hoped this confrontation wouldn't happen. She just wanted to finish the week without incident but she could not turn her back on patients. She had the skills and she would be damned if she would let Matthew prevent her from practising medicine.

'You've been here five minutes and you take on a surgical case. We have two surgical residents!'

'I know that, but Dr Sanderson is still on leave and Dr Ericson took the other case.'

'It didn't cross your mind to call for me or a consultant?'

Beth wasn't taking kindly to his rebuke. She had acted professionally and competently and the surgical procedures were well within her abilities.

'There wasn't time. I had severed arteries to consider, not hospital politics.'

'Following hospital guidelines has not been your forte since you arrived, though, has it, Dr Seymour?'

Her patience was quickly wearing thin. She was doing her best to be civil. She had tolerated his unfair allocation of cases, but the patient's life was more important than his pettiness.

'Did he die?' she asked bluntly.

'Not yet,' he retorted with equal animosity. 'But it's early days. He's still in Theatre.'

'If that's all, I'll be going. I'm sure there's a sprain or rash I need to see.'

The tension was unbearable but she had only another two days until she could leave. Her heart was heavy; she still loved Matthew but he was not accepting her decision. She wondered if he ever would.

She wondered for a moment if perhaps she was being foolish.

Could she really get back all of those years that Charlotte and Hattie had stolen from her? Was she being naïve? Was she trying to live in the past? She had told Matthew not to live in the past, but was this not what she was doing? But she couldn't stop her need to turn back the clock, despite the cost.

Everyone in A and E was aware of the tension between the two but no one knew why. Beth thought it was best left that way, and from Matthew's apparent silence on the matter, she assumed he had made the same decision.

Dan had given up on Beth and Matthew making up and he actually felt sorry for Beth. She had been taking the brunt of Matthew's mood for two days and he couldn't understand the sudden shift from Beth being the favourite to being ostracised and punished. She wasn't saying anything. The obstetric resident had asked for a transfer back to his ward and another resident reluctantly arrived in A and E. He appeared to be visibly shaking.

Matthew finally caught up with Beth in the corridor late in the day.

'I wanted to speak to you about something that's been brought to my attention and I was wondering whether you would mind accompanying me to my office.'

Beth swallowed hard as she fell into step, making her way down the corridor to his office.

He closed the door behind them before he began. 'Your paperwork arrived. Dr Lancaster did the legwork for you.'

Beth just nodded. He had the paperwork in his hands and it was self-explanatory.

'So, Dr Seymour, when are you off, then?'

'I'm leaving the Eastern at the end of tomorrow's shift and flying out Friday morning at ten. I'm hoping that I can return to the programme in a month or so, when I come back.'

Matthew stared coldly and then, with a self-satisfied smirk, delivered a message Beth had not expected to hear. 'Afraid not. The resident exchange programme has been closed as of today. Had a word in Lancaster's ear and explained that you arriving and leaving had caused a great disruption to the running of A and E and I thought we should put the programme on hold until we could have an evaluation of the benefits to the hospital and staff.'

He crossed the room and sat down behind his desk. He was using every ounce of strength not to break down and tell her how he felt. Instead, he steeled himself and pretended he didn't care.

'That's it, then?' Her voice rose. 'I need to return to England and you decide that's enough of a reason to close down the programme? I don't get consulted about whether I might want to return?'

Matthew paced the floor behind his desk. He was angry and hurt in equal proportions. He wanted to grab this woman and shake her to her senses and tell her how much he loved her. But he couldn't. Beth had made her choice and he had to push her so far away she would never come back.

'No. And I'm afraid I haven't had time to write a reference.' With that he crossed the floor and stormed out of the room.

CHAPTER TEN

MATTHEW BECAME INCREASINGLY reclusive over that day and the next. It was like he had given up on arguing with anyone and everyone.

Dan was happy that the relentless nit-picking had died down but worried that Matthew seemed lost in his own thoughts. While still functioning, he seemed preoccupied. Dan thought he looked drawn and tired. Almost battle worn. Or broken-hearted.

'Hannibal has almost gone AWOL on us,' he said in passing.

Beth didn't comment. She was still reeling from Matthew's hurtful behaviour. She knew what he was doing and why. He was angry and he was disappointed but this was her life and her family and her decision.

Dan was scribbling a prescription for a patient when he paused and looked at Beth. 'I don't know what happened or didn't happen between you two, but our beloved leader is not coping with you leaving.'

'Rubbish,' Beth retorted with a sigh. 'He'll be glad to see the back of me. I imagine he'll send an armed escort to the airport to make sure I leave.'

Dan shook his head. 'You can't see it, Beth, but the man is a shell now. He's barely functioning. There's no fire in him. I think I prefer the unreasonable psycho boss to this pathetic individual who's running the show like his dog just died in front of his eyes.'

'You're imaging things, Dan.'

Dan crossed the waiting room, handed the script and gave instructions to a young mother with her toddler in tow. He walked back to Beth, still deeply concerned about Matthew but not wanting to dampen Beth's happiness about leaving. 'Truly, Beth, he's not okay about you going. But it's not your problem and if I were you I'd be off and running tomorrow with bells on after what he's put you through.'

Beth walked off to take a well-earned break but Dan's words resonated in her mind. She didn't believe them but they made her wonder what was really going on with Matthew. He had kept his distance since their heated discussion in his office and seemed almost depressed. She couldn't work out what would have caused this change but she was very sure it wasn't her leaving Eastern Memorial. He had made sure she couldn't return, so clearly he didn't intend to try to work things out.

She would almost bet he'd plan a fireworks display to celebrate the end of the exchange programme after she left, if the hospital budget would allow it.

The day drew to a close without any emergencies. It was a quiet end to her penultimate day. There was no sign of Matthew. He had made himself even more scarce, leaving the staff to run A and E. She knew if there was an emergency he would be on call but he chose to stay in his office. Better for everyone, she mused as she put her coat in her locker. One more day and she'd be off and running.

The next morning Beth woke with mixed emotions. She lay in her bed staring at the ceiling, thinking about everything that had happened over the last crazy month. It had been an emotional roller coaster. She had been so excited when she'd arrived in Adelaide, bright-eyed and full of enthusiasm for this next phase of her life. With no idea of what to expect, except warm weather and loads of sunshine, she had wanted to embrace this change as an adventure. This would be a turning point in her life that would bring opportunities to grow professionally and personally. She had experienced a fairly sheltered upbringing and after her mother's death a lonely one. She had learnt to stand on her own two feet but still within the family confines, and this had been her chance to become her own person.

This had been her chance to make her mark and grow. She'd wanted to make her father proud and knew deep down that she'd wanted to make him notice her again. But more importantly she'd wanted to be true to herself and find the field of medicine that suited her best. She'd known that if she'd stayed in London she would have been drawn to vascular surgery and she hadn't been sure whether that was her dream or whether she had just been trying to please her father.

Adelaide was supposed to have helped clarify where she belonged and what challenged her and made her most happy and fulfilled. A and E had certainly felt right. And being with Matthew had felt right. How wrong had she been?

Beth rolled over and looked at her clock. It

was time to get ready for the last day at Eastern Memorial. She wasn't sure what it would hold for her but she just wanted it over.

Her first patient for the day was an elderly woman with suspected kidney stones. She had presented at Reception with her daughter-in-law complaining of pain coming in waves, lasting between twenty minutes to an hour, beginning in the lower back and radiating to the groin. She had been vomiting, had a fever and small amounts of blood in her urine.

'It's so very painful, my dear,' she began in barely more than a whisper. 'I kept poor Bert up all night with it. He's ever so worried.'

'I'm sure he is, Mrs Saunders. But we will find out exactly what the problem is so that Bert can stop worrying.'

Beth obtained a urine sample and sent it straight to the lab for urinalysis. She also asked Yvette to arrange for her patient to be sent for an ultrasound to confirm her diagnosis.

'I believe you may have a kidney stone,' Beth explained to Mrs Saunders and her daughter-in-law. 'I need to have the results back from the test on your urine and the ultrasound before I can confirm it, but it may have grown to a size that can't be passed in the urine stream. But let's get that pain under control first and then you'll be taken for your ultrasound.'

Beth signalled to Yvette. 'I need eight hundred milligrams of ibuprofen immediately and we'll need that repeated three times a day if Mrs Saunders is admitted. I can see by the notes that she has private cover so she may like to transfer to a private hospital after we have decided on the treatment. I'm assuming the mass is over three millimetres to be causing the pain, so there will need to be some type of intervention.'

Beth turned her attention back to her patient and daughter-in-law. Removing her gloves, she took the elderly woman's hand in her own. 'If the stone is too large to pass, and I'm assuming it is because of the pain you're in, we may have to look at methods to either shatter the stone into smaller fragments, using a process called extracorporeal shock wave lithotripsy, or we might have to operate. But let's leave that until we have a clearer picture of what we're dealing with. But you will be fine and back home with Bert as soon as possible.'

'We've been married for fifty-three years and we've never been apart for more than a few days. And that was only because I was in hospital, having my only son, Martin.' She looked warmly at her daughter-in-law. 'Alice is married to Martin, you know, and he's very lucky to have her.'

Beth smiled at the pair and could see what a wonderful relationship they enjoyed.

'Are you married, my dear?' Mrs Saunders asked.

'No, but I hope to be one day.'

The elderly woman took the medication and water that Yvette handed her, and with Alice's assistance swallowed the tablets.

'I highly recommend it.'

Beth smiled at her. 'I think it would be lovely to be with one man for fifty-three years.'

Beth didn't see Matthew observing her at the entrance to the examination bay. She turned to see his eyes narrow, before he walked away without saying a word.

'My, he was a bit nice, that young doctor. Tall and rather good looking,' Mrs Saunders said with a wicked smile. 'I can see why you would enjoy working here. Lots of husband material around.'

Beth shook her head at the thought. Matthew wasn't relationship material, let alone husband material. He had slammed the door on the possibility of her returning to the hospital and to him. It was over and he had made sure she would never come back.

The orderly suddenly appeared at the entrance to the bay where Matthew had been standing and broke into Beth's reverie. He had arrived to take Mrs Saunders for her ultrasound. The elderly woman thanked Beth as she was wheeled out of A and E.

'We'll see you back here a little later and talk about your treatment,' Beth told her.

'And we can talk some more about that lovely young doctor,' she said with a smile. 'Don't want to leave it too long to find a nice husband.'

Beth smiled at her but the woman's words cut like a knife. Taking a deep breath, Beth put her thoughts of Matthew as far away as she could and faced the rest of her last day.

She was grateful A and E was busy all day and before she knew it she had finished her final shift at Eastern Memorial and said farewell to the team. Beth had declined the after-work drinks that Dan and Yvette had suggested as a farewell. She wasn't up to pretending she was happy about leaving. The idea of toasting the time she had spent at Eastern Memorial did not sit comfortably with her. She bought them all some chocolates in her lunch break to thank them for their support and assistance. She felt confident she had made some great friends and she promised to visit Adelaide again one day in the future. And made them promise that if they ever travelled to England, they would come and stay. She had initially hoped to return to Adelaide and the Eastern Memorial to work, but since Matthew had closed the exchange programme so swiftly, Beth wasn't sure where her future lay. She might just stay in England and work for a while. She wasn't thinking much beyond her trip home and leaving the future open. She might look into other exchange programmes in Australia, if Matthew didn't witch-hunt them all into closure in her absence. She accepted that he could stop her working at the Eastern but he couldn't prevent her visiting the friends she had made Down-Under. They were like family to her now.

Matthew approached Beth as she was walking towards the doctors' lounge to collect her belongings from her locker.

'Dr Seymour,' he began, and then he paused for the longest moment looking at the woman who stood before him. Her examination coat was creased and splattered with iodine, her hair was falling in unruly curls from her ponytail, her make-up was barely there and the little that was around her eyes was smudged. Yet he still thought she was beautiful. He didn't want to, but he did. She had obviously been on her feet all day and looked like she needed a long bath and a good night's sleep…in his arms. 'Beth, here is your reference. I think you will find it is a fair and accurate report. You will be an asset to any hospital.' He held out an envelope for her.

He had written a glowing report. It was an honest account of her ability to carry out her duties as a resident in A and E. She had broken his heart but she was a great doctor and he couldn't take that away from her. She knew how to operate as part of a cohesive team, she worked well under pressure and she had real empathy for her patients. He wasn't about to destroy her professional future despite how he felt about her as a person.

Beth was surprised that he would actually have taken the time to write a reference. She couldn't understand how he could have been so cruel and cold for the past three days then give her this. He wasn't looking at her with the contempt she had seen recently. He seemed different. Beth wasn't sure if this was an olive branch but she was happy to end her time at the hospital on pleasant terms.

'Thank you, Matthew. I really do appreciate the reference.' She wished with all her heart everything had turned out differently.

Matthew nodded and walked away without saying another word.

Beth suddenly felt empty. She knew this was not logical. Matthew didn't want a relationship. He didn't care about her. He was unreasonable, short-tempered and stubborn. He was devoid of empathy for her family situation. But for some inexplicable reason Beth knew she still loved him. It made no sense and as she watched him disappear into his office she knew she had to forget him, however long that took.

Matthew sat in his office with the door closed. He felt like his world was collapsing around him. He remembered the feeling of loss when he'd found out that Anne had disappeared into the night without a word, but this felt worse, much worse. He loved Beth more than he'd thought he could ever love anyone. The thought of never seeing her again was weighing heavily on him and consuming his every thought. He had been doing the bare minimum to keep A and E running and decided he would take extended leave after Beth left the hospital.

He needed to take a break and look at his

life. Only a few short days ago he had been lying in Beth's bed, thinking that life couldn't get any better. He'd had the woman of his dreams in his arms and he'd thought they would build a life together. They would settle down and maybe one day even have their own family. Now he was alone. He had his work but even that was not enough any more. Beth had given him so much joy and brought him back to life and now she was leaving. And he couldn't stop her.

He was lost.

He didn't know where to turn. His role at the hospital wasn't enough any more. The joy he felt around Beth made everything else seem insignificant. He remembered the oddest things, like wiping the froth off her lips with his handkerchief, how gorgeously dishevelled she'd looked at the end of a long shift, and the warmth of lying in her bed. Her beautiful face kept haunting him. He would just have to bury himself in his work like he had for the last five years. Good, reliable work. He could depend on that to always need him and always be there.

He turned off the light in his office and slowly made his way to his car. He looked around, hoping to see Beth waiting for a cab. He knew he couldn't offer her a lift home but he just wanted to see her gorgeous smile once more before she left. There was so much that had gone unsaid. He knew that he would never get to talk to her the way they had when they'd been alone, neither would he hold her in his arms, but he wanted more than anything to see her once more, even from a distance. But she had gone and so had his chance to be with the woman who had captured his heart totally.

Beth had finally finished packing the last of her belongings. The day had been uneventful as she'd prepared for her return to London. She had hoped Matthew would understand her need to go. His reaction was beyond anything she had expected. Closing the programme meant ending any chance for them.

She had taken a long walk into the city and out again through the parklands. The idea of sitting in her maisonette all day until she left for the airport was not a good one. Her thoughts would be on what might have been and where it had all gone wrong. There was nothing she needed to buy, so she had a coffee. She couldn't eat. Her stomach was churning. She had so much to think about. Her decision to leave on a minute's notice was weighing on her heavily. Was Matthew right? Was running back to her father a mistake? The walk was to keep her busy and her mind from wandering back to all that Matthew had said. And all that Matthew was.

Was she making the biggest mistake of her life in leaving for England?

Her travel documents were safely packed in her hand luggage with the reference from Matthew. She reached in and pulled out the envelope. Running her fingers lightly over her name that Matthew had written in bold print on the front, she thought back to the moment he had handed it to her. He'd looked almost remorseful. Perhaps he was sorry for what had transpired. Beth would never know what he was thinking, she realised, but she was grateful at least that he had written the reference. She chose not to read it as she thought it might be painful and bring the tears back again just before the cab arrived. Slipping it back into her bag, she decided it was reading material for after her arrival back in England.

The cab was due in twenty minutes. She looked around the room. Against her will, she pictured Matthew lying on the sofa. She remembered back to that night and how she had eagerly and without hesitation taken him by the hand from the sofa to the warmth of her bed. Looking back to her bedroom, the door was ajar and she could see the freshly made bed. She remembered how messy it had looked after they had spent the night together. Their clothes lying discarded on the floor. The sheets tangled around them when she'd woken up. Looking at her bedroom was more painful than she thought possible.

She brought her eyes back to the lounge room. But there were memories there as well. The vase that had held the dozen perfect yellow roses now stood empty on the table. It was washed and clean, awaiting blooms from the next tenants. Yellow roses were apparently not a symbol of new beginnings at all, she thought. At least, not for her.

She saw her suitcases packed and standing by the front door. It wouldn't be long now, she mused, before she could fly to Sydney then board the long-haul flight home to England and leave the hurt behind. And begin the hard task of putting Matthew out of her mind. She had thought only a matter of weeks ago that this would be her home for a long time. That Matthew Harrison would be her future and that life was so wonderful. How wrong she had been.

CHAPTER ELEVEN

'FINAL BOARDING CALL for flight QF seven-three-six to Sydney. All passengers, please make your way to Departure Gate nine.'

Matthew stood staring in silence at the empty departure lounge. He felt physically ill. There was no sign of Beth. She was gone. Suddenly he heard footsteps behind him and turned in hope, only to see a red-faced young man running into the lounge, waving his boarding pass. The flight attendants scanned his boarding pass and then followed the flustered passenger down the walkway, closing the entrance behind them. Matthew walked towards the huge window with the plane in full view. He thought that she might still be in the walkway and if she turned round she would see him. But she wasn't there. He pictured her fastening her seat belt and readying herself for the first flight of her journey back home.

Matthew dropped into the nearest seat with his head in his hands. He was so angry with himself for not fighting harder. For not being more honest with Beth about his feelings. She had been so warm and loving and she'd given him no reason to doubt her, but his stupid insecurities and pride had made him think the worst of her. She had crept inside his heart but he knew at every opportunity she had tried to get close he had been the one to run. And now it was too late.

'Are you okay, mate?' came a stranger's voice.

Matthew looked up and managed to mutter, 'Yeah, I'll be fine.'

'Airports are tough going on the emotions sometimes,' the man replied, then picking up his carry-on luggage he walked over to his family. Matthew watched him warmly greet a woman with a kiss and then scoop up a little girl into his arms, kiss her on the forehead and walk away with both of them towards the exit and out of sight.

Matthew wanted more than anything at that moment to be that man, being greeted by a loving family. But he knew that he had given Beth no reason to believe he would be a family man. She had every right to doubt his ability to commit to a relationship at all.

He was more disappointed than he'd thought possible. She had slipped through his fingers. Beth was gone and there was not one damn thing he could do about it.

Not thinking about much more than putting one foot in front of the other, he made his way to the airport car park. In his mind, and in his heart, the outcome had played out so differently. He had imagined stopping Beth from boarding the plane and promising to love her forever. Her telling him that she felt the same way.

He drove home picturing her face and her beautiful smile. He hoped that she would find peace with her family when she returned to London. And more than that, he hoped that one day she would find a place in her heart for the time they'd had together.

A and E was buzzing when he returned. There was nowhere else for him to go. Home would have most definitely sent him mad with his regrets and the emptiness he felt to the core of his very being.

He didn't greet anyone and with his head down he made his way to his office to collect his white coat. It would be a long day, he thought as he swung open the door.

'Matthew,' a familiar voice said softly from the other side of the room.

'Beth?' He stood staring at the woman before him. 'I thought you'd left for Sydney.'

'I changed my flight. I had to talk to you.'

Matthew crossed the room. He just wanted to grab her and hold her.

'Please, Matthew,' she said firmly, keeping him at arm's length. 'I need to say some things and know how you feel, honestly feel.'

A slight frown crossed Matthew's brow. He was so happy to see her. He couldn't believe she was really there standing in the same room. But there was distance in her voice and he couldn't ignore it. 'Sure.'

'You know I fell for you, even though you are a very complicated man,' she started, and then crossed to the window and looked out intently over the hospital gardens. 'I thought I knew what I was getting into. Stupidly I believed the chemistry we shared would get us through anything.' She turned back and looked at Matthew with tears welling in her eyes. 'But you and I both have some baggage. We have issues that we're still sorting through…'

'We can do it together,' he offered as he nervously ran his fingers through his hair and paced his side of the room. It was as if she had drawn an invisible line down the centre. 'You don't have to face anything alone if you don't want to. I've been stupid and pig-headed. I don't want to lose you, Beth.'

Beth wanted to believe him. She had changed her flight because she didn't want to make the biggest mistake of her life. She wanted with all her heart to know if Matthew could accept her need to see her father without fireworks, accusations and suspicion. Now, tomorrow, whenever she needed to go back to England. It couldn't ever be this hard again. If he couldn't accept it then she was prepared to accept that it was over.

'I need to see my father. Maybe he doesn't deserve my time. Maybe he does. Perhaps I've overreacted over the years and expected too much of them,' she said, crossing the room and sitting back down on the small sofa where her handbag rested. 'I just know my father finally needs me. He needs *me*. And that's something I've waited years to hear.'

Matthew heard the pain in her voice.

'But you thought the worst apparently,' Beth continued, as she bit her lip to stop the tears. 'And you are right, he did have twenty-eight years with me, and the last eighteen weren't the best. But I want to see if he can be that man I looked up to again. I just need this time with him again.'

'I overreacted. I know that now, Beth,' Matthew answered her as he moved closer to the line she seemed to have drawn across the room. 'I admit I don't know if I'd bother and I guess it's why I reacted the way I did. I didn't understand you leaving me for them after they had treated you badly. I was scared, Beth. I was scared of losing you, but I pushed you away to protect myself. I didn't want to be the victim again. I thought I'd rather be the bastard who ended it than a poor pitiful son of a bitch left waiting and never having you return. But that was just wrong and I regret it.'

Beth fidgeted nervously with her handbag. 'I need to ask you something honestly.'

'Anything.'

'Can you look at me and tell me that you can put the hurt Anne inflicted behind you? Can you trust that if I say I want to be with you, I mean it? That I won't spend my life paying for her mistake? That if I want to visit my father or friends back home there won't be the Spanish Inquisition? I don't want to have you thinking all the time that I will up and disappear because our lives aren't perfect. I'm better than that. I would never turn my back on you even if life deals us hardship or obstacles.'

Matthew knew that doubting Beth was the biggest mistake he had made. She'd never given him reason to think she was anything like Anne. Beth was strong and loyal.

'I can leave it all behind, I swear. You made me believe in love again and I have to stop carrying around the hurt. It's got no place in my life if you're with me.'

Beth felt a weight lifting from her. She was so glad she had swallowed her pride and changed her flight.

'What about you? Do you want to see where this can go?' he asked, as he took her hand and held it in the warmth of his.

Beth looked at the man sitting beside her and knew without hesitation that she did but only if she would have space to make decisions. She had been doing it for herself for so long.

'I do,' she began, taking a deep breath, 'but—'

Her sentence was silenced with a kiss. A tender, passionate kiss that sent her pulse racing. 'That's all I need to know, the buts can be worked out.'

'Are you sure?' she said, still a little breathless from the kiss. 'I'm used to making my own decisions, I'm not sure I want to ask you about everything I might want to do.'

'I don't want you to ask permission, I want to be your lover and your best friend. I just want to share your life and I want you to lean on me sometimes. I want you to be there when I wake up. I love you, Beth. God knows, I've tried not to. I've tried to drive you away but I can't. I've spent five years on my own, with work as my only constant companion, and I've been just fine, but since I met you I don't want to be alone any more.'

Beth looked away, still a little scared that these were just words.

'I want you to go to London. Spend time with your father and know that I will be here. I will wait, and if he isn't the man you hoped he would be, we'll get through that too. You will never be looking for attention with me around.'

Beth smiled. 'You truly don't mind if I go?'

'I have to set you free and believe in my heart you will come back.'

Beth's mouth curved to a soft smile. 'I will be back, I promise.' She leaned closer, leaving no space between them.

'I love you, Beth. I think I started to fall in love with you the very first day I met you

and now I just don't want to live a day without you—'

Beth leant over and silenced Matthew's
words with a kiss.

'I love you too.'

EPILOGUE

THE DAY OF the wedding couldn't have been more perfect. The spring sky in Adelaide was as brilliant a blue as the groom's sparkling eyes.

George had travelled from London with Beth to walk her down the aisle. She wore a beautiful strapless gown of cream silk taffeta, a shoulder-length veil and her mother's pearl choker and earrings.

George knew in his heart that Beth had made the right decision in moving Down Under but he felt remorse for the circumstances that had forced her to do so. Their time on the Amalfi Coast had allowed Beth to open up about her loneliness when she'd been growing up. He regretted that he had been so caught up in keeping his new wife happy that he hadn't seen Beth's sadness. He'd promised to make it up to her. He was so very proud of Beth and the woman she had become, and he told her how equally proud her mother would be, looking down on this special day. He knew if it took him the rest of his life he would prove to her he could be the father she needed and deserved.

St Peter's Cathedral in North Adelaide was picture perfect with posies of yellow roses and angel's breath on the end of each pew. As George had filed for divorce, Hattie hadn't been invited to the wedding. Beth had, out of courtesy, invited Charlotte. However, she was suffering from hyperemesis gradivarum. Pregnancy had been the impetus for her sudden wedding. The severity of the morning sickness had meant that she couldn't manage the long flight to Australia. She wasn't missed by anyone.

Yvette and Sylva were absolute visions in strapless jade silk cocktail dresses, but Matthew was not impressed with the attention Dan was giving his sister. He would sort that out when he returned from honeymoon. He could tolerate the woolly-headed young man at work but definitely not in his family.

Edward Lancaster was the master of ceremonies at the lavish luncheon reception held in a large marquee decorated in white and soft daffodil organza in the garden of his beautiful home. Edward and Dorothy spent the entire function trying to convince George to move to Australia. There was a definite need for his skills and knowledge and by the afternoon's end he had decided to relocate. He selfishly hoped that he would be able to spend time with his grandchildren one day if he too lived Down Under.

Beth couldn't have been happier. She loved the man beside her at the wedding table with all her heart and she knew he felt the same. He moved even closer and she felt his warm breath on her neck.

Matthew's powerful arms encircled her and, to the tapping of the guests' knives on the crystal glasses, his mouth met hers with a tender kiss.

Beth was overwhelmed by her desire to be alone with him. 'By the way, I've switched off your pager, Dr Harrison. You're not getting out of my sight tonight. The Eastern Memorial will have to survive without you.'

He kissed her into silence, then moving his lips only inches from hers he murmured, 'I don't want to be away from you for a second. Not tonight, or any other night for the rest of our lives.'

* * * * *